"*The Adventures of Nanny Piggins* is the most exciting saga about a flying pig nanny ever told. There is a laugh on every page and a lesson in there somewhere. I recommend it highly."
— Madeleine K. Albright, former U.S. Secretary of State

"Like my favorite chocolate cake, Nanny Piggins is totally irresistible! This book is sweet, surprising, and makes me hungry for more. Delicious!"
— Peter Brown, *New York Times* bestselling author of *The Curious Garden*

★ "Mary Poppins, move over — or get shoved out of the way. Nanny Piggins has arrived.... This is smart, sly, funny, and marvelously illustrated with drawings that capture Nanny's sheer pigginess."
— *Booklist* (starred review)

"Readers looking for nonstop giggles and cheerful political incorrectness will devour this as quickly as Nanny Piggins can consume a chocolate cake."
— *Publishers Weekly*

"Reluctant and avid readers alike will get caught up in this book's humor, charm, and adventure."
— *School Library Journal*

NANNY PIGGINS
AND THE WICKED PLAN

By
R. A. Spratt

Illustrated by
Dan Santat

LB
LITTLE, BROWN AND COMPANY
New York   Boston

Text copyright © 2009 by R. A. Spratt
Illustrations copyright © 2012 by Dan Santat
Text in excerpt from *Nanny Piggins and the Runaway Lion* copyright © 2010 by R. A. Spratt

Little, Brown and Company

Hachette Book Group
1290 Avenue of the Americas, New York, NY 10104
Visit us at lb-kids.com

Little, Brown and Company is a division of Hachette Book Group, Inc.
The Little, Brown name and logo are trademarks of Hachette Book Group, Inc.

The publisher is not responsible for websites (or their content) that are not owned by the publisher.

First U.S. Paperback Edition: July 2013
First U.S. hardcover edition published in July 2012 by Little, Brown and Company
Originally published in 2009 by Random House Australia Pty Ltd.

Library of Congress Cataloging-in-Publication Data

Spratt, R. A.
Nanny Piggins and the wicked plan / by R. A. Spratt ; illustrated by Dan Santat.—1st U.S. ed.
p. cm.
Summary: When Mr. Green announces his diabolical plan to remarry, his children are horrified at the thought of losing their beloved Nanny Piggins.
ISBN 978-0-316-19923-0 (hc) — ISBN 978-0-316-19922-3 (pb)
[1. Nannies—Fiction. 2. Brothers and sisters—Fiction. 3. Pigs—Fiction. 4. Humorous stories.] I. Santat, Dan, ill. II. Title.
PZ7.S76826Nan 2012
[Fic]—dc23
2011027061

10 9 8 7 6 5 4 3 2

LSC-C

Printed in the United States of America

Book design by Saho Fujii

THANK YOU FOR BUYING *Nanny Piggins and the Wicked Plan.* It is a very good book. You have made an excellent decision. But before we get into the actual adventures, Nanny Piggins has insisted that I explain a few things. So, for all those people who have not read *The Adventures of Nanny Piggins*, or for those people who have read it and subsequently suffered amnesia after a nasty blow to the head, I will now tell you who everyone is and what is going on.

In the first book, Nanny Piggins (the world's most glamorous flying pig) ran away from the circus and came to live with the Green family as their nanny. The Green children— Derrick, Samantha, and Michael—fell in love with her instantly. Who could not fall in love with a nanny whose only job qualifications were her astonishing ability to be fired out of a cannon and her tremendous talent for making chocolate cake, sometimes both at the same time?

Derrick, the oldest, is a conscientious boy, although a little on the scruffy side. Samantha, the middle child, is a worrier (and, living with Nanny Piggins, there is quite a lot to worry about). And young Michael is a happy spirit who enjoys a slice of cake almost as much as his nanny does.

Mr. Green was, at first, reluctant to hire Nanny Piggins because he could not get over the fact that she was a pig. But as Nanny Piggins pointed out, human nannies are extremely overrated, being greedy and not terribly clean.

Also, she only charged ten cents an hour. So being a man with no morals, Mr. Green hired her on the spot—although he did leave the NANNY WANTED sign out in his front yard, still hoping to hire a suitable human nanny when the opportunity arose.

Nanny Piggins and the Green children have had some wonderful adventures, including the arrival of Nanny Piggins's brother, Boris, the ballet-dancing bear. Boris is ten feet tall, weighs over one thousand pounds, and comes from Russia, so he is very in touch with his emotions. You may be wondering, "How can a pig have a bear for a brother?" Well, that is a long story (which you can read in *The Adventures of Nanny Piggins*, Chapter Eight), but the short answer is: adoption.

And that is it. That is all you need to know. There is also a ringmaster, a hygiene-obsessed rival nanny, a silly headmaster, thirteen identical twin sisters, and lots of other characters. But you will find out about them as you go along. So why not fix yourself a snack, snuggle up somewhere comfortable, and enjoy this book?

Yours sincerely,
R. A. Spratt, the author

To Violet

ACKNOWLEDGMENTS

I would especially like to thank…

Mum & Dad
Elizabeth Troyeur
Esther Perrins
Connie Hsu
Linsay Knight
Chris Kunz
Nerrilee Weir
Mick Molloy
and
the wonderfully supportive librarians of America

CONTENTS

CHAPTER ONE

Mr. Green's Wicked Plan

M r. Green rolled up his sleeves and inspected his tools. He had a crowbar, a pickax, a long-handled shovel, and a chain saw all laid out on the ground in front of him. He was not sure which to use. He was not a man who was used to manual labor, because he was a lawyer, so he never did any real work. Certainly not work that involved his hands.

Meanwhile, across the street, Nanny Piggins, Derrick, Samantha, Michael, and Boris (the dancing bear) all crouched hidden in Mrs. Pumpernickel's azalea bushes watching Mr. Green.

"What's he up to?" whispered Michael.

"He's not gardening, is he?" worried Samantha. She was sure her father's idea of gardening would involve killing all the plants and pouring concrete over everything.

"Perhaps he's digging a grave," suggested Derrick.

"Hmm," said Nanny Piggins, because she was too busy watching to say anything more complicated.

"Look! He's putting on gloves!" exclaimed Boris, who had a better view than anybody else. Being ten feet tall, his head stuck out above the azalea bushes.

"And he's picking up the chain saw!" exclaimed Michael.

"He *is* a murderer!" exclaimed Derrick.

"No, look!" exclaimed Samantha. "He's going for the sign!"

And sure enough, Samantha was right. There had been a sign standing in the Greens' front lawn for many months. It read "NANNY WANTED: ENQUIRE WITHIN." And Mr. Green was now approaching this sign while revving the chain saw.

"I can't watch," squealed Boris, who was very sensitive.

With a roar of the chain saw, Mr. Green sliced through the wooden stake that held the sign aloft, then stood back and watched as the weather-beaten placard flopped facedown on the lawn.

"Do you know what this means?" asked Samantha, clutching her nanny joyously. "He's stopped looking for a human nanny."

"He doesn't want to replace you anymore!" said Michael, taking out a celebratory chocolate bar.

"You're going to be our nanny forever!" exclaimed Derrick.

"Hmm," said Nanny Piggins. She did not like to dampen the children's enthusiasm, but she had known Mr. Green for many months now, and it had only taken her three seconds to accurately gauge his character. So she suspected he had a less happy reason. "Children," said Nanny Piggins, "I think your father might be up to something."

And that was, indeed, the case. Mr. Green *was* up to something. And even though Nanny Piggins and the children had tremendous imaginations as a result of reading an awful lot of trashy novels, even they could not have imagined the wickedness Mr. Green had in mind.

It was all revealed the next morning at breakfast. The Green family was gathered around the breakfast table, except for Boris. (Mr. Green had not yet realized there was a giant dancing bear living in his garden shed, so Boris still had to stay hidden. At breakfast time he sat outside the window and Michael passed out slices of honey-covered toast to him. Fortunately, not only had Mr. Green failed to notice the ten-foot bear in his garden, he also had not noticed that he was paying for fifty gallons of honey to be delivered to the house every week. He was not an observant man.) Everyone was eating breakfast quietly, waiting for Mr. Green to leave, when he disappointed them by clearing his throat.

That could only mean one thing. He was going to talk to them seriously about something. Samantha and Derrick stifled a groan. Michael groaned outwardly.

And Nanny Piggins shoved seven jelly-filled doughnuts in her mouth and braced herself for the worst.

"As you know, your mother has been dead for some time," began Mr. Green. (Not a pleasant conversation starter, I think you will agree. But Mr. Green was not a sensitive man.)

"Two years, three months, and five days," supplied Derrick.

"And eleven hours," added Samantha.

Michael didn't add anything; he just whimpered.

"And of course I miss her," continued Mr. Green. "I miss having someone to do my laundry, cook my meals, and fetch my dry cleaning."

"So you've decided to buy a slave?" asked Nanny Piggins as she tried to both hurry Mr. Green up and guess where this conversation could possibly be going.

"No," said Mr. Green, pausing for no reason. (He always left long pauses in the middle of sentences. It's a trick lawyers use because they charge their clients by the hour, so if they speak slowly they get paid more.) "I have decided to get married."

"What?" yelled Derrick.

"No!" hollered the normally quiet Samantha.

"*Mpf*," spluttered Michael because he had just been hit in the face with seven partly chewed doughnuts spat out in shock by Nanny Piggins.

"To a woman?" asked Samantha, just to be sure, because she was finding it very hard to wrap her mind around the idea. The children could never understand why their own mother had married Mr. Green. They just assumed she had taken too much cold medication that day, or been hit on the head by a falling air-conditioning unit, or something (they watched a lot of cartoons). It had never occurred to them that their father might find another woman who was equally temporarily insane.

"Who is she?" asked Nanny Piggins, deciding to immediately ring the poor woman and try to talk her out of it.

"I haven't met her yet," said Mr. Green.

"Oooh," said Nanny Piggins and the children with a huge sigh of relief. They were pleased that it was just Mr. Green who was insane, not some poor woman. They all seriously doubted that Mr. Green could ever find anyone crazy enough to marry him.

"But I do have a date," added Mr. Green.

Now this amazed them.

"With a woman?" asked Nanny Piggins, just to be sure.

"Of course," spluttered Mr. Green.

"All right, no need to be species-ist," said Nanny Piggins, who had never understood what humans saw in each other.

"Does she have bad eyesight?" asked Michael. He felt it would be easier for his father to trick someone who could not see him.

"Her name is Miss Pettigrove, and she works at our firm," explained Mr. Green.

"So she's a lawyer?" asked Nanny Piggins. She was having visions of an awful female version of Mr. Green.

"No, she's a cleaning lady," said Mr. Green.

"A cleaning lady!" exclaimed Derrick, Samantha, and Michael. They were astonished.

"Yes," said Mr. Green. In fact, it was her ability to clean that had drawn his admiration. Mr. Green, like any man, was attracted to tall, beautiful blonds. But he was even more attracted to a woman who would set to work at five o'clock in the morning and make a linoleum floor shine until you could see your face in it. He had not seen his face in his own kitchen floor for years. Two years, three months, and five days, to be exact.

Nanny Piggins and the children sat there in stunned silence. They did not know what to think, so they certainly did not know what to say. Nanny Piggins had even stopped eating (her jelly doughnut poised in front of her agape mouth), she was so shocked.

But Mr. Green had not finished. He had something else to add. He cleared his throat to regain his family's attention.

"So, er..." said Mr. Green. (He always struggled to know how to ask for something. Nanny Piggins said it was because he must have had all his charm surgically removed as a child.) "So, um..." continued Mr. Green, "I will be needing you, Nanny, er...Piggins, to do me a favor."

"Really?" said Nanny Piggins. She loved it when Mr. Green asked for favors. It almost always resulted in him buying her a cake.

"I intend to take Miss Pettigrove on a picnic," said Mr. Green. (He had planned a picnic because it was cheaper than going to a restaurant.) "So..." he continued, "I will need you to look after her baby."

"She has a baby?" queried Nanny Piggins. This was most unexpected.

"Yes, she's a widow," explained Mr. Green.

"Then shouldn't she be *Mrs.* Pettigrove?" asked Samantha.

"I suppose so," said Mr. Green. He had never really thought about it. The truth was, not only did Mr. Green have Miss Pettigrove's title wrong, he had her name wrong as well. Her name was really Mrs. Pettigrain. But Mr. Green was the type of man who did not think something like his cleaning lady's actual name was important. "Anyway, she'll be arriving here in—" Mr. Green looked at his watch—"three minutes, so I'll need you to babysit the child for the rest of the day."

"I don't know," said Nanny Piggins. "We were going to get started on inventing a perpetual motion machine by going down to the garbage dump to look for bicycle wheels. If we did this 'babysitting,' what would we get in exchange?"

"Er...the pleasure of helping me out?" suggested Mr. Green.

The children rolled their eyes. Nanny Piggins shook her head sadly. "You'll have to do better than that."

Mr. Green looked terrified for a moment. He thought Nanny Piggins was about to ask for a raise. But then he remembered all his previous negotiations with his nanny. "I could buy you a cake?" he suggested hopefully.

"A chocolate mud cake that is three feet wide!" demanded Nanny Piggins.

"One foot wide," countered Mr. Green. (He enjoyed negotiating.)

"Six feet wide!" said Nanny Piggins.

"Um, I'm not sure you understand the principles of negotiating," said Mr. Green.

"Nine feet wide!" demanded Nanny Piggins.

"All right, all right," said Mr. Green, realizing it was better to give up now. (He never enjoyed negotiating with Nanny Piggins.)

"Deal!" exclaimed Nanny Piggins.

The children cheered and Nanny Piggins sprang across the table happily to shake Mr. Green's hand. After all, how hard could babysitting a baby be? But Nanny Piggins's self-congratulation and excitement were soon interrupted by a terrible wailing noise.

"What on earth is that dreadful noise?" asked Nanny Piggins.

No one had time to answer because the doorbell rang. And the children were too busy running to the living room to peek out the window and see the woman crazy enough to go out with their father.

Mr. Green insisted on opening the front door himself, which meant that they all had to watch him being nice to Mrs. Pettigrain. It was cringe-worthy. It was not so much what he said—they were perfectly normal things like "Hello, how are you, do come in"—but it was the way he said them, all smirking and preening. (Mr. Green rarely tried to be pleasant; as a result he was not very good at it.)

Mrs. Pettigrain was not at all what they'd expected. She was small and thin, with worn old clothes. And she looked both sad and frightened at the same time. This surprised the children. Their father was usually obsessed with appearances, so they realized he must be very keen on having his floors waxed to think it was a good idea to date such an unimpressive-looking lady.

Meanwhile, the wailing continued.

"Where is that dreadful noise coming from?" Nanny Piggins asked the children as she shoved pieces of doughnut in her ears to block out the sound.

"It's the baby," explained Samantha, pointing to the stroller Mrs. Pettigrain had left in the corner of the room. (Being the girl, she instinctively knew these things.)

"Has the baby swallowed some kind of police siren?" asked Nanny Piggins.

"No," explained Derrick. "The baby is crying." (Being the oldest, he was a font of information.)

"Does it have to do it so loudly?" asked Nanny Piggins. Nanny Piggins was not a great one for crying herself, unless something really terrible happened. Like someone eating the last piece of chocolate cake. Or her trotter[1] getting painfully caught in a vending machine when she was trying to return a health bar and swap it for the chocolate bar she really wanted.

"Babies always cry like that," said Michael. And he would know because he was only seven years old, so

---

[1] A trotter is a pig's foot. When Nanny Piggins found out that I had referred to her feet as *hooves* in my first book, *The Adventures of Nanny Piggins*, she was very angry with me. Apparently, she finds the word *hoof* inelegant and insulting, and I had wounded her pigly pride. In fact, she stomped hard on my foot, just to clear up any confusion I might have had about what a trotter was. From this point on, I will always refer to Nanny Piggins's feet as trotters.

he was the one who had most recently been a baby himself.

"We'll see you at four o'clock," said Mr. Green as he grabbed Mrs. Pettigrain firmly by the hand and whisked her out of the house before Nanny Piggins had a chance to reconsider their agreement.

Nanny Piggins and the children found themselves left alone with the baby. They peered in over the edge of the stroller. The baby looked very red in the face and unhappy as it screamed louder than anything that small had a right to be able to scream. "Well, the first thing we need to do is stop it from making that awful wailing sound," said Nanny Piggins. "Wait here."

Nanny Piggins hastily disappeared into the kitchen. A moment later she reappeared, carrying a huge slice of chocolate mud cake, saying, "This ought to cheer it up."

"No!" yelled the Green children in unison. Fortunately Derrick was able to grab Nanny Piggins's wrist and Samantha was able to put her hand in front of the baby's mouth before Nanny Piggins could jam the cake in there.

"What's wrong?" asked Nanny Piggins. "Do you think it would prefer coffee cake?"

"Babies this age don't eat cake," explained Michael.

"They don't?" asked Nanny Piggins, with genuine surprise. "Then what do they eat?"

"They only have milk," explained Samantha.

"Surely not," said Nanny Piggins. "Surely you mean they only have milk chocolate."

"No, Samantha's right," added Derrick. "Babies only drink milk."

"No wonder they are so unhappy and cry all the time," said Nanny Piggins with genuine sympathy. "The poor little things. Aren't they even allowed hot chocolate? That's got milk in it."

"No, just plain milk," said Samantha firmly.

Now Nanny Piggins felt like crying, she felt so sorry for the little baby. "But how do we get it to stop crying?" she asked, thinking it would be worth at least trying the chocolate mud cake on the baby, because having bits of jelly doughnut shoved in her ears was getting sticky and unpleasant.

"Babies like being hugged," suggested Derrick.

"Really?" said Nanny Piggins. This brightened her up. "Michael, run and fetch Boris."

"Why?" asked Michael.

"Because he's a bear. And all bears are experts at hugging," explained Nanny Piggins. "That's why they named the bear hug after them."

Michael soon returned with Boris.

"What is that dreadful noise?" asked Boris. He wasn't very experienced with babies either.

"This poor baby is upset because it can only drink milk," explained Nanny Piggins.

"Yuck!" said Boris.

"I know," said Nanny Piggins. "Apparently it needs a hug."

"Don't we all," said Boris as he carefully scooped up the little baby. He personally believed there should be much more hugging in the world.

"You're not going to crush the baby, are you, Boris?" asked Samantha. She loved Boris dearly, but he did sometimes forget how huge and strong he was.

"Don't be silly," said Nanny Piggins. "You wouldn't ask Einstein if he knew how to add. You wouldn't ask

Mozart if he could hum a tune. So you shouldn't question a bear's ability to hug."

Boris held the helpless little baby close to his chest, surprisingly tenderly for a one-thousand-pound, ten-foot-tall bear, and rubbed it soothingly on the back. Miraculously, the baby stopped crying.

"You see!" said Nanny Piggins, as she deftly ate the baby's slice of mud cake. "Now we'd better get started with the babysitting. I suggest we take turns. I'll go first. Put the baby on the sofa, Boris, and I'll start sitting on it right away."

Fortunately the Green children were, again, able to grab Nanny Piggins before she actually sat on the infant.

"What's wrong?" she asked.

"You don't actually sit on a baby when you babysit," said Derrick.

"You might squash them if you did," added Michael.

"Babysitting just means baby-watching," explained Samantha.

"Then why do they call it *babysitting*? They really should name it better or there could be some terrible accidents," said Nanny Piggins.

"Eggs like being sat on," Boris reasoned. "And they're baby birds. Are you sure this baby wouldn't like to be sat on, just for a minute or two?"

The Green children lunged to stop Boris as his bear-sized bottom moved dangerously close to the baby.

"No, we're definitely just meant to watch after the baby," insisted Derrick.

"A whole day with a baby. We'll have to think up something to do with it," said Nanny Piggins thoughtfully.

"I think most babysitters just sit and watch television while they're taking care of the baby," said Samantha, starting to worry what her nanny might have in mind.

"I'm sure we can come up with something better than watching television," said Nanny Piggins as she looked at the baby closely. "It is a remarkably pretty baby."

Indeed, as they all looked closely at the baby, they had to admit, it was very pretty. It did not look at all squashed and blobby like so many babies do. And now that her skin was fading back to a nice pink, after the

17

bright red it had turned from crying, she was looking positively lovable.

"What could possibly be better than watching television?" asked Michael, genuinely baffled.

"I know!" exclaimed Nanny Piggins. "Starring on television!"

And so, three hours later, Nanny Piggins, the Green children, Boris, and the baby were sitting in the waiting room of a talent agency.

"Are you sure this is a good idea?" worried Samantha. She was pretty certain Nanny Piggins should ask Mrs. Pettigrain's permission before signing up her baby to be in a television commercial.

"Of course it's a good idea," said Nanny Piggins. "If this baby could talk, she would thank me. Every woman should get a job as soon as possible. Because jobs mean money, and money means not having to rely on anybody else to buy you chocolate cake. Remember that, children."

"But she doesn't look like any of the other babies here," pointed out Derrick.

And he was right. All the other babies waiting with their mothers in the waiting room looked immaculate. They were wearing cute little outfits, and cute little bows in their cute little hair. Even the mothers looked cute. As if they had all been ironed, then driven to the audition lying down so as not to get creased.

The Pettigrain baby, on the other hand, looked completely different. Nanny Piggins had not intended to make the baby dirty when they left the house. But on the way to the audition, they had passed a large puddle of mud that Nanny Piggins, being a pig, found impossible to resist. And she knew the children, particularly Derrick, loved being dirty. So she ordered them and the baby to play in the mud immediately. Nanny Piggins thought very highly of the medicinal benefits of mud. To her mind, rolling in mud was a great way to cool off, moisturize the skin, and clean off any excess soap that might have built up on the body. So they spent a full hour doing that.

Then, because rolling in mud was hungry work,

they had all stopped for ice cream. And Nanny Piggins managed to get ice cream all over the baby's face before the Green children could grab her and convince her that babies do not eat ice cream either.

Then there was the honey. Boris had just happened to be eating from a five-gallon tub of honey when the baby started crying. And being a very kind-hearted bear, he immediately gave her a big bear hug without washing his hands first.

So as the Pettigrain baby sat in the waiting room, she looked very happy, but also extremely dirty, sticky, and brown.

The other mothers were giving Nanny Piggins and the baby sidelong looks of disgust. This did not bother Nanny Piggins. She was used to prejudice. She had suffered a life of pigism, so dirtism was no surprise. She knew humans, particularly clean humans, could be very narrow-minded.

"Pettigrove," called out a young man carrying a clipboard.

"That's us," said Nanny Piggins.

Nanny Piggins, Boris, and the children trooped into the audition room with the baby. It was a large room with a desk in the middle. Behind the desk sat a director, a casting agent, and a young woman operating a video camera.

"Pettigrove," said the director without even looking up. "What's the baby's first name?"

"I don't know," admitted Nanny Piggins. "Nobody told us. We call her Baby."

The director looked up from his paperwork and was immediately dumbstruck. Amazingly, he was not staring at the elegantly dressed pig, the ten-foot-tall bear, or the three mud-covered children, but the Pettigrain baby herself.

"That's it! She's perfect!" he exclaimed.

"She is?" said Michael.

"Of course she is," said Nanny Piggins.

"Finally someone has come to this audition properly prepared," said the director with delight.

"We have?" queried Derrick.

"All the other mothers have been bringing in their pristine, clean babies. Whereas your baby is filthy and disgusting," said the director with a huge smile on his face.

"And that's a good thing?" asked Samantha.

"All the other mothers have been bringing in their pristine, clean babies. Whereas your baby is filthy and disgusting."

"Of course it's a good thing," said the director. "We're advertising baby cleaning wipes, so we need a baby who knows how to be utterly filthy and love it."

They all turned to look at the Pettigrain baby cooing happily in Boris's arms. There was no denying that underneath the caked-on layers of filth, she certainly looked very happy indeed.

················· ★ ★ ★ ·················

Later that afternoon, Nanny Piggins, the children, and Boris were all in the living room playing Lava Floor (where you jump from one piece of furniture to another pretending that the floor is made of deadly boiling lava) when Mr. Green and Mrs. Pettigrain returned. Mr. Green looked very smug. He had been out on a six-hour date and only spent $2.50 on an ice cream for himself (but not one for Mrs. Pettigrain, saying he knew "how ladies like to watch their weight"). Mrs. Pettigrain, on the other hand, looked even sadder and more miserable than when she had arrived that morning. The only thing that cheered her up was seeing her baby and giving her a bear hug.

"Good technique," whispered Boris from his hiding place behind the curtains. "Not bad for a human."

"So how did you get on?" asked Mr. Green. Not that he really cared, but he thought it made him look good to have a conversation with his staff.

"We got the baby a job," said Nanny Piggins. "It's going to be paid twenty thousand dollars to be in a television commercial for baby wipes."

"Twenty thousand dollars!" exclaimed Mr. Green, wishing he had a ring so he could get down on his knee and propose to Mrs. Pettigrain right away. He dearly wanted a wife to scrub his floors. But a wife with a baby who could bring in an even greater hourly rate than a tax lawyer was too good to be true. Unfortunately for Mr. Green, however, he never got a chance to propose.

Mrs. Pettigrain was too busy squealing with delight, dancing for joy, and kissing her baby.

"We're rich, we're rich, we're rich!" she cried. "Now I don't have to go on any more dates with horrible, unattractive, middle-aged men who are too cheap to even buy me an ice cream."

"I beg your pardon?" said Mr. Green, which was

really rather stupid because there was no way he was going to enjoy hearing Mrs. Pettigrain repeat herself.

"I only went out with you because I felt I owed it to Melissa to find her a father," said Mrs. Pettigrain.

"Ahhh, Melissa, that's her name." Nanny Piggins nodded. "I thought she looked like a Melissa."

"I know a widow living on a cleaner's wage can't afford to be picky," continued Mrs. Pettigrain. "But the mother of a television commercial star can be very picky indeed."

And so Nanny Piggins's first attempt at babysitting an actual baby ended very happily. Mrs. Pettigrain was happy she did not have to marry a horrible man like Mr. Green. Baby Melissa was happy to spend a whole day rolling in mud for the commercial. And Nanny Piggins, Boris, and the children were happy because Mrs. Pettigrain gave them a 10 percent commission for getting the baby the job. And they spent all the money on having five tons of mud deposited in Mr. Green's garden, where they had a wonderful time rolling about, getting every last smear of soap off their bodies.

CHAPTER TWO

Nanny Piggins and the Tunnel to China

It all started with Nanny Piggins reading the most brilliant pirate story ever. She became so absorbed in the book that she could not put it down, not even for meals. Derrick, Samantha, and Michael had to feed Nanny Piggins snacks while she kept her eyes glued to the pages. The only time she took a break was at the end of each chapter so she could act it all out for the children and Boris. They loved this bit.

Nanny Piggins was very good at acting out novels. She did all the voices, all the silly walks, and all her own stunts. Her demonstration of Captain Bad Beard's attack of the *Good Ship Lollipop* was spectacular. It involved swinging from the living room chandelier with a spatula between her teeth before savaging her imaginary enemy. (Suffice to say, Mr. Green's ottoman would never be the same again.) So when Nanny Piggins finished the pirate book, they were all very sad.

"I wish we were pirates," said Nanny Piggins wistfully. "Pirate life has so much going for it: battles, seafood, and, best of all, treasure."

"It's almost as glamorous a job as being a nanny," said Boris.

"I know," agreed Nanny Piggins. "You children should really consider piracy. Do they ever ask pirates to come and speak to you at your school's career day?"

"No," admitted Derrick. "They usually just have accountants come and tell us how accountancy is really exciting."

"They let people come and lie to you?" asked Nanny Piggins. "Your headmaster is a very immoral man. Still, I suppose you don't need career advice to become a pirate — you just run away to sea."

"But the truancy officer gets upset when we don't

go to school," said Michael. "So I'm sure she'd get really upset if we ran away to live a life of crime on the high seas."

"She's such a spoilsport," sighed Nanny Piggins. (Nanny Piggins did not think much of the truancy officer. She was diabetic, so Nanny Piggins could not bribe her with cake.) "I'm sure you'd learn more as a pirate. After all, pirates need to know how to sew sails, tie knots, and blast cannons at passing ships. Now that's much more practical than that 'math'"—Nanny Piggins always said *math* as though it were a swear word—"they insist on teaching you at school."

"And, I bet they don't have to wash every day," mused Derrick. "Nanny Piggins is right. We should become pirates!"

"What?!" worried Samantha. After all, she was a shy girl. She did not like talking to strangers, let alone attacking them on the open ocean.

"We all have to get jobs eventually, so why not take up piracy now?" he continued.

"We'd learn lots of geography, oceanography, and the importance of avoiding scurvy," piped up Michael.

"And I really like those puffy shirts pirates wear," added Boris.

"Then that's decided. We're all becoming pirates. What do we do first?" asked Derrick.

"We need treasure," declared Nanny Piggins.

"But where are we going to find treasure?" asked Michael. "Father doesn't even give us pocket money, so he's never going to give us treasure."

"Treasure isn't something you get given," explained Nanny Piggins. "It's something you dig up. It's always buried."

"Why?" asked Samantha. It was bad enough she was becoming a pirate, but now it seemed she was doomed to have dirty fingernails as well.

"Because pirates never open bank accounts. They don't like filling out forms," said Nanny Piggins.

"But where are we going to find buried treasure?" asked Michael.

"In the ground, of course," said Nanny Piggins patiently. "There's probably lots buried in the back garden right now."

"Really?" said Derrick.

"There's only one way to find out," said Nanny Piggins.

And so Nanny Piggins rang the school and said that all three Green children had been struck down with a case of twenty-four-hour smallpox. Then they set to work being pirates. The first thing they needed was the right clothes, so Nanny Piggins took them up to Mr. Green's bedroom and plundered his wardrobe. He had very boring clothes, but with some dye, permanent markers, a pair of scissors, and a sewing machine, Nanny Piggins was soon able to turn one of Mr. Green's best suits into five excellent pirate costumes.

Then they went out into the garden with their spades.

"Where do we start?" asked Derrick as he looked around his father's garden for a likely spot.

"In pirate stories, *X* always marks the spot," reasoned Nanny Piggins. "So the first thing we shall have to do is make an *X*, then dig beneath it!"

And that is exactly what they did. Nanny Piggins marked an *X* right in the middle of Mr. Green's perfectly tended lawn (which had only just been professionally restored after having had five tons of mud dumped on it—see Chapter One), then immediately started hacking up the turf with her spade.

It soon became clear that Nanny Piggins was really good at digging for treasure. Thanks to all the cake she ate, she had boundless energy. Once the spade was in her trotters, she just dug and dug and dug. The children tried to help, but they could not keep up. And Boris kept shrieking and jumping out of the hole every time he saw a worm. So Nanny Piggins put them all in charge of supplies (fetching cake) and keeping watch for enemy pirates (the truancy officer), and that arrangement worked well.

By midmorning Nanny Piggins had dug a very, very deep hole—so deep she could not climb out of it. The children had to make a rope ladder out of Mr. Green's neckties to get her out in time for morning tea.

As they sat in the sun and ate their chocolate chip cookies, Nanny Piggins, Boris, and the children were very happy. Being pirates had been very satisfying so far. Really, there was just one problem. "You haven't had much luck finding treasure," Michael politely pointed out. They all looked at the small pile of things Nanny Piggins had found in her hole. It consisted of three buttons, a spoon, an apple core, a Frisbee, and the handle from a teacup.

"What are you talking about?" protested Nanny Piggins. "I've found three buttons! They'll be invaluable next time your trousers start falling down."

"But you haven't found a chest full of gold and jewels," pointed out Derrick. "That's what pirates always look for in books."

"I suppose," conceded Nanny Piggins, who, nevertheless, still felt proud of her buttons.

"Why don't you try digging somewhere else?" suggested Derrick, hopeful that they might get the next day off school as well.

"Well, it seems a shame when this is such a good hole," said Nanny Piggins. "I might as well keep going with this one."

"Why?" asked Samantha. She liked a hole as much as the next girl, but it seemed to her that it was plenty big enough.

"I'm starting to get peckish," explained Nanny Piggins, "so I thought I'd keep digging all the way through the center of the world until I end up in China. Do you fancy some Chinese food?"

The Green children loved Chinese food, so they agreed this sounded like an excellent plan. (They had set out for Chinese food some months ago, but high seas and colliding with a Korean fishing boat had delayed them.) The children were not entirely sure whether burrowing through the center of the earth was the quickest way to get to China. But China was certainly a long way away, and the earth was round. So through the ground was undeniably the shortest route.

Nanny Piggins finished her morning tea and kept on digging. She dug and dug and dug, for day after day. Although not all in a straight line. After day two she found it too hard to keep digging straight down because there was too much rock in the way. So Nanny Piggins started digging sideways instead.

On day three, the truancy officer came and dragged the children back to school. Apparently you are not allowed to quit school and become a pirate until you are sixteen, even if you do have a signed permission slip from your nanny.

And on day four, Boris had to go because he had promised to teach ballet to vagrants down at the YMCA.

So Nanny Piggins had to continue with her hole

alone. Until, suddenly, on the eighth day of digging, her spade hit a piece of stone that gave way, and on the other side she could see a light. Nanny Piggins was very excited. A light could mean only one thing—she had tunneled all the way through to China!

Nanny Piggins hacked more rock out of the way to make the hole bigger, then wriggled out through the opening into the foreign and exotic land. But when she looked about, Nanny Piggins was startled to discover that China was not at all how she'd expected it to be. She was expecting a great big country with Chinese restaurants in every direction as far as the eye could see. In reality, China was just a very large room with forty men all hanging around, playing cards, and lifting weights.

"Hello," said Nanny Piggins, because she had forgotten to learn Chinese. Fortunately the Chinese men seemed to understand English, because they all looked up and stared at her. They were naturally surprised to find a filthy pig dressed as a pirate suddenly arriving in their country.

"What do you want?" asked the biggest and scariest of the men as he stood up and loomed over Nanny Piggins.

But when she looked about, Nanny Piggins
was startled to discover that China was not
at all how she'd expected it to be.

"Oh good, you speak English," said Nanny Piggins. "Could I have some Chinese food please?" She was not at all scared. She was prepared to pay for the food. She had found two quarters down the back of Mr. Green's couch just the other day.

"What?" demanded the scary-looking man in a very unfriendly manner.

Nanny Piggins looked around. He was not the only man in the room who looked unfriendly. Most of the men were frowning, some were scowling, and one man in the corner was nervously biting his nails. They all looked unhappy. Nanny Piggins could see these men needed help. Luckily, being a circus pig, she knew just how to cheer them up — with a show!

And that is just what she gave them. After three hours of her best tap dancing, followed by knife juggling and fire breathing, the men were delighted. They were calling for more. They even sent someone to the kitchen to whip up some chow mein for her, so she would have enough energy for an encore.

Many hours later, Nanny Piggins returned to the Green house with wonderful stories about the hospitality of the men in China.

Derrick and Samantha were naturally suspicious. They knew their nanny was an amazing woman. And they were sure that she was capable of tunneling much farther than any other nanny. But they had studied some geography at school, so they were not entirely convinced that even Nanny Piggins could dig all the way through the center of the earth to China in just eight days.

"Are you absolutely sure it was China?" worried Samantha. (She was not sure what to worry about, but the situation was making her feel a general, all-purpose worry.)

"Of course," said Nanny Piggins.

"Did it look like China?" asked Derrick excitedly.

"What does China look like?" asked Nanny Piggins, because pigs are lucky enough to not be forced to study geography.

"Did you see the Great Wall of China, the Entombed Warriors, Tiananmen Square, or anything like that?" asked Samantha.

"Did they have dim sum?" asked Michael, knowing that his nanny was more likely to have noticed food.

"I didn't see any of those things. But there was a big gray room with lots of men in it," said Nanny Piggins.

"I suppose that could be China," conceded Samantha. "They have gray rooms and men in most countries."

"Why don't you come and see for yourselves tomorrow?" suggested Nanny Piggins. "After all, it will be a wonderful educational opportunity for you to experience a different culture, and going to school one day a week should be more than enough to satisfy the truancy officer."

"Would we need to take our passports?" asked Samantha.

"Do you have passports?" asked Nanny Piggins.

"No," admitted Derrick.

"Then you'd better not bring them," reasoned Nanny Piggins.

At ten o'clock the next morning, Nanny Piggins rang the school and said that Derrick, Samantha, and Michael had come down with twenty-four-hour bubonic plague. Then they all climbed down into the tunnel and set out for China.

On emerging from the other end of the hole, it became immediately clear to the Green children that there was, indeed, no need for passports. Because they were not in China. They were in a maximum-security prison.

"We're going to be in so much trouble," wheezed Samantha as she started to hyperventilate. She had suspected that Nanny Piggins would land them all in jail one day. But she had thought it would be through doing something wrong, not through digging a tunnel and voluntarily climbing in.

"What are you talking about?" Nanny Piggins was puzzled. "We're in China. Why would we be in trouble?"

"This isn't China," explained Derrick.

"Are you sure?" asked Nanny Piggins. "I ate some lovely chow mein here yesterday."

"This is a prison," explained Michael.

"A what-son?" asked Nanny Piggins.

"A place where the government locks up bad men," explained Michael.

"They lock up bad men?" asked Nanny Piggins. This took her by surprise. In her opinion the government had the most peculiar ways of doing things.

"Yes, people who steal or cheat on their taxes or hurt other people get locked up," explained Michael.

"Then why isn't your father in prison?" asked Nanny Piggins.

The children had to think for a moment. It was a good question.

"Because he's never been caught," suggested Derrick.

"Prison seems like a very drawn-out way of punishing people. When I'm cross with someone, I just bite them on the leg. And if I'm really cross, I bite them on both legs," said Nanny Piggins. Not that she needed to tell the children. They had seen the teeth scars on their father's calves. (Unlike the government, she had caught him many times.)

"Are you going to tap dance for us again, Nanny Piggins?" asked Phillip, who was serving two years for stealing his grandmother's wheelchair and taking it for a joyride.

"No, you were such good hosts last time I visited, I just popped in to see if you'd like to share morning tea at our home," said Nanny Piggins with her most gracious hostess smile.

"What?!!!" exploded Derrick and Samantha.

Michael did not say anything. He was too busy rushing back up the tunnel to hide his teddy bear.

"You can't invite them over," said Samantha with some difficulty because she was trying to talk out of the side of her mouth while still smiling at the men.

"Why not?" asked Nanny Piggins.

"Because they're prisoners. They aren't allowed to leave," explained Derrick.

"Piffle. I'm sure no one will mind if we bend the rules a little," said Nanny Piggins.

"But that's the whole point of prison. You have to stay in no matter what," said Samantha.

"Even if there's a half-price chocolate sale at the supermarket?" asked Nanny Piggins.

"Even then," confirmed Derrick.

"They must be very wicked men to get such harsh punishment," marveled Nanny Piggins. "Still, it's important to be polite. Always remember, children, there is no greater crime than rudeness. They hosted me, so I must invite them over." Nanny Piggins turned and loudly addressed all the men. "Would you all like to come and visit us for morning tea?"

"Yes, please!" said all the prisoners.

"Nanny Piggins!" exclaimed Derrick.

"They're prisoners," pleaded Samantha.

"You'll promise to come back here again afterward, won't you?" asked Nanny Piggins.

"Of course," said the prisoners.

"But the guards will notice that they're gone," argued Samantha.

"That's okay. We'll leave a note letting the guards know where we are," said Nanny Piggins. "They can't complain about that."

Derrick and Samantha suspected that the guards could indeed complain about that, but there was no time to discuss it further. Nanny Piggins was already shepherding prisoners into the tunnel ahead of her and telling them to put the kettle on when they got to the house so she could make them some hot chocolate.

It took the children a while to relax about having forty convicted felons in their home, but once they did, even they had to admit that the morning-tea party was a success. When Nanny Piggins found out that they did not have sticky buns in prison (the most severe part of their punishment), she immediately set to work. In a tornado of flour, sugar, butter, and jam, she soon whipped up the most gloriously delicious sticky buns ever. The prisoners enjoyed them so much it brought tears to their eyes. Mikey, the check forger, swore to give up crime altogether if she would give him the recipe.

After they had eaten, Boris performed a special ballet dance for them. He had not meant to, but he was stung by a wasp (which is what can happen when you let jam get all over your fur). Boris did some of his most spectacular flying leaps and pirouettes. Then, after the applause had finished, Nanny Piggins reenacted a story from her pirate book. It was a particularly good one that involved swinging on the curtains, then having a pretend sword fight up and down the mantelpiece. So naturally they all lost track of time. That is, until Nanny Piggins looked at the clock and screamed, "Aaaaggggh!"

"What's wrong?" asked Derrick.

"It's twelve o'clock! On the note I'd promised I'd

have all the prisoners back by eleven forty-five," replied Nanny Piggins.

"We're going to be in so much trouble," worried Steve (who was serving time for impersonating a parking inspector).

"The guards don't like it when we're late for lunch," added Bruce (who was serving twelve months for poisoning his brother's potted plant).

"Don't worry," said Nanny Piggins. "If you quickly hurry back along the tunnel, perhaps they won't have noticed you're gone."

"Good idea," said Steve.

And so all forty prisoners rushed out into the backyard and over to Nanny Piggins's hole. But they did not jump in, because someone was waiting for them.

Standing at the bottom of the pit was a very angry-looking man.

"Who's that?" asked Nanny Piggins. "And why is he in my hole?"

"It's the warden," whispered Steve. "He's in charge of the prison."

"Hello," said Nanny Piggins, optimistically adding, "Would you like a sticky bun?"

But the warden just ignored her and yelled directly at the prisoners. "I'm personally going to see to it that all of you have your sentences tripled! Digging an escape tunnel and breaking out is unforgivable. But to do it right before lunch, when Chef has been slaving all morning over a lovely casserole, is despicable. You should be ashamed of yourselves!"

The prisoners all hung their heads.

"I wish he wouldn't yell," said Boris, who, being a sensitive bear, had hidden in the compost heap.

"But it's not their fault, sir," interrupted Nanny Piggins. "They didn't dig the tunnel out. I dug the tunnel in."

The warden turned to look at Nanny Piggins. He had never been interrupted by a pig before, let alone one so glamorous, but he was too cross to let that affect him. "*You* dug the tunnel?!" he roared. "You organized this mass breakout from my prison?!"

"Yes," admitted Nanny Piggins truthfully.

"Then I'm going to see to it that you go to jail for fifty years!" exclaimed the warden.

The Green children were horrified. Fifty years was an enormously long time to be without their beloved nanny. Who would bake them cakes? Who would help them shred their homework? Who would teach them how to install a hydrogen engine on a skateboard? And they knew there was no chance of Nanny Piggins's getting out early for good behavior. Good behavior was not her strong point.

"All right," said Nanny Piggins calmly.

"All right?!" exclaimed the children. Surely their nanny could not be giving up that easily.

"If you'll just step into the house for a moment while I powder my nose," said Nanny Piggins.

Now the children knew Nanny Piggins was up to something. She never talked about "powdering her nose." If she was going to the toilet, she would say, "I'm going to the toilet." Apart from anything else, she did not have a nose; she had a snout. So they followed her into the house to see what would happen next.

"While you're waiting," suggested Nanny Piggins to the warden, "have a sticky bun."

Now these sticky buns looked particularly delicious (Nanny Piggins's baked goods always did). Even a professionally miserable man like the warden found them hard to resist. There was snowy-white icing sugar on top, then thick, gooey cream as well as great big globs of strawberry jam inside, so altogether it was too much for any man to resist. Especially a man who'd only had oatmeal for breakfast.

"I am feeling a bit peckish," he admitted.

By the time Nanny Piggins returned from pretending to "powder her nose," the warden was polishing off his seventh sticky bun. There was icing sugar and jam all over his face, and a big dollop of cream on his tie.

"These sticky buns are spectacular," gushed the warden.

"I know," said Nanny Piggins, because she was always truthful but rarely modest.

"And this hot chocolate is so...so...so chocolaty," added the warden.

Which made Nanny Piggins blush with pride, because really, there is no greater compliment.

"It's just a shame I can't invite you over to morning tea again," said Nanny Piggins.

"You can't?" said the warden. He looked like he was going to cry.

"No, if I'm serving a fifty-year jail term, I doubt

I'll find the time to make sticky buns," said Nanny Piggins.

"Oh," said the warden.

"And I won't get to be in your prison," continued Nanny Piggins. "I'll be in a women's prison."

"Oh," said the warden again.

Everyone in the room—all forty prisoners, Derrick, Samantha, and Michael—looked at the warden expectantly.

"I suppose you don't necessarily have to go to jail," began the warden.

"I don't?" asked Nanny Piggins innocently.

"Breaking into a prison isn't nearly as bad as breaking out of one," continued the warden. (He could be quite reasonable when his blood sugar was high.)

"The only thing is," said Nanny Piggins, "I suppose I'll have to fill in the hole."

"There's no rush to do that," said the warden.

"There isn't?" asked Nanny Piggins.

"You might as well leave the hole there. As long as all the prisoners promise not to use it to escape," said the warden.

"You promise, don't you?" said Nanny Piggins.

"Oh yes, we promise," said the prisoners. (They did not want their sticky-bun route filled in either.)

"Then I don't see what harm one little tunnel causes," said the warden.

"Excellent!" exclaimed Nanny Piggins. "Then you can all pop in for chocolate mud cake next Thursday."

And so Nanny Piggins was very satisfied with her time as a pirate. She had visited China and made forty-one new friends. But best of all, she had a great big hole in the garden ready to push Mr. Green into the next time he annoyed her.

CHAPTER THREE

The Duel at Dead Man's Gorge

Nanny Piggins and the children were on their hands and knees recarpeting the living room. I know this sounds like a very industrious thing to do. But I should explain that the only reason they were recarpeting the room was because they had tested to see if sulfuric acid really would burn a hole through the floor, like they had seen in a movie. And their experiment had been one hundred percent successful.

Having completed the experiment, however, it then

occurred to them that Mr. Green might not be too impressed with the results. He seemed to be inordinately fond of his bland brown floor covering. He always lost his temper if anyone made a mud slippery slide over it or ground custard pie into the fibers. So having tried and failed to hide the hole with a vase of flowers (the three-hundred-year-old antique vase simply dropped through the hole and smashed in the basement), Nanny Piggins decided on recarpeting.

Fortunately, they found a piece of carpet that fit perfectly — it was lying on the floor of Miss Smith's living room. She was an elderly spinster who lived across the road. They borrowed Miss Smith's carpet (without asking). I know this sounds an awful lot like stealing, but really it was just borrowing. Nanny Piggins was perfectly prepared to return the carpet if it ever occurred to Miss Smith to ask her whether the carpet stapled to their floor was her own.

As luck would have it, this never became an issue. When Miss Smith returned from bingo at the church hall and discovered that her living room was now carpetless, she was delighted. She thought some Good Samaritan had polished her floorboards. And because

Miss Smith loved ballroom dancing, floorboards were much better as far as she was concerned.

So Nanny Piggins, Derrick, Samantha, and Michael were just stapling down the last corner of Miss Smith's bright purple rug, using Mr. Green's desk stapler, when they heard a pounding at the front door.

"Who could that be?" asked Nanny Piggins.

"It can't be the truancy officer," said Michael. He knew this for a fact because he had seen the truancy officer sprain her ankle earlier that morning, while chasing Nanny Piggins through Mrs. Lau's vegetable patch.

"No, she could never have healed this quickly," agreed Nanny Piggins. "Unless she is part cyborg, which would not surprise me at all."

"Perhaps it's a door-to-door salesman," suggested Samantha.

"No, they don't come anymore," said Nanny Piggins sadly. "You bite one salesman and they all hold it against you."

"He brought it on himself," comforted Derrick. "He promised to make your whites whiter. If he is going to tell fibs, he deserves to suffer the consequences."

The pounding at the door started up again.

"Well, there's only one way to find out who it is," said Nanny Piggins. "We'll just have to peek through the window."

"Or we could always answer the door," suggested Samantha.

"Oh yes, I suppose we could try that too," conceded Nanny Piggins. "It would be quicker."

And so, without peeking through the window, the letter flap, or the keyhole, or using the spy camera attached to the roof, Nanny Piggins flung open the front door to see who was there and immediately regretted it. For there on the doorstep was an angry-looking armadillo. (Now if you do not know what an armadillo looks like, I had better describe it. Because an armadillo is the type of animal that, if no one told you what it looked like, you would never guess. It is most peculiar. It looks like a pig going to a costume party dressed as a tank. Like a pig, an armadillo has short legs and a snout. But unlike a pig, an armadillo is covered in a leathery, hard shell.) Then the armadillo, without any introduction or explanation, immediately tried to slap Nanny Piggins across the face with a glove.

Fortunately, however, Nanny Piggins was an eighth-degree black belt in taekwondo. Her self-defense reflexes were so superfast, she could not have let an armadillo slap her in the face even if she wanted to. She just blocked the slap. The armadillo tried to slap her again and again and again. But each time Nanny Piggins deftly blocked the blow.

"Would you just hold still and let me slap you, for goodness' sake!" said the exasperated armadillo.

"Why?" asked Nanny Piggins. She could not see any good reason she should let an armadillo slap her, but she was prepared to be open-minded.

"Because I'm trying to challenge you to a duel," said the armadillo.

"You're what?" asked Nanny Piggins, beginning to believe that armadillos were as peculiar as they looked.

"Oh, I understand," said Samantha.

"You do?" said Nanny Piggins, Derrick, and Michael in unison, because they certainly didn't.

"In the olden days, if you wanted to challenge some-one to a duel, you slapped them in the face with a glove," explained Samantha.

"Did you learn that at school?" asked Nanny Piggins, begrudgingly beginning to feel the first dawning of respect for the education system.

"No, I learned it from reading lots of historical romance novels," admitted Samantha.

"Then it must be true," decided Nanny Piggins, because she had a lot of respect for romance writers.

"The child is correct," declared the armadillo. "My name is Eduardo Montebianco, and I have traveled all the way from Mexico to challenge you to a duel."

"Why?" asked Nanny Piggins.

"Did you steal his true love or dishonor his family name?" questioned Samantha. "That's the reason they usually have duels in novels."

"I don't think so," said Nanny Piggins. "But I am very glamorous. Sometimes I have a powerful effect on people without even realizing. Once, the head coach of the Chinese gymnastics team saw me being fired out of a cannon and was so impressed with my athleticism and grace, she immediately went home to China and made all her gymnasts put on fifty pounds by eating doughnuts."

"Did it improve their performance as gymnasts?" asked Michael.

"No. They enjoyed the doughnuts so much, they all ran away to open doughnut shops," admitted Nanny Piggins. "But they were very happy."

"I'm challenging you to a duel," interrupted Eduardo, "because you claim to be the greatest flying animal in all the world."

"So?" said Nanny Piggins, perfectly confident that this was true.

"It is a lie," declared Eduardo. "For I am the greatest flying animal in all the world."

Now if you are paying attention, you might, at this point, question how either a pig (Nanny Piggins) or an armadillo (Eduardo Montebianco) could possibly claim to be the greatest flying animal in all the world when there are so many animals that have wings—for instance, birds. But you have to understand, for circus folk, a flying animal that uses wings is just cheating. It would be like the bearded lady sticking a toupee to her chin, or the trapeze artists wrapping themselves in Bubble Wrap in case they fell, or the strong man getting a friend to help him lift things. When Nanny Piggins and Eduardo talked about the greatest flying animal, they both meant the same thing—being fired out of a cannon. Which is something to boast about because being fired out of a cannon is really difficult, whereas flapping wings is really simple, if you've got them. Now, back to the story.

Nanny Piggins's eyes narrowed. "You?" she said, managing to compact an enormous amount of contempt into that one short word.

"Yes, I," said Eduardo. "For I too belong to a circus. And I too am fired out of a cannon. And it offends me to have a mere woman, and a mere pig, claiming to be better than me."

"Really?" said Nanny Piggins, as she looked over the armadillo from head to toe, trying to decide which part of him she was going to bite first.

"Yes, really," said Eduardo. "So I challenge you to a duel, to prove once and for all that I am the greatest animal aviationist alive."[2]

"Okay," said Nanny Piggins, deciding that the armadillo's plated shell looked too difficult to bite, and that she would have to be content with punishing him another way. "Where and when?"

---

[2] This is just a showing-off way of saying *flying animal*.

"Tomorrow morning at dawn," declared Eduardo.

"Fine," said Nanny Piggins, even though, in her opinion, the only decent thing to do at dawn was sleep.

"We shall align our cannons side by side, then fire them to see who goes the farthest," continued the armadillo.

"All right," said Nanny Piggins. It sounded simple enough to her.

"And to make things interesting," added Eduardo, "we will fire our cannons across"—he paused here for dramatic effect—"Dead Man's Gorge!"

"No!" gasped all three Green children.

"What's Dead Man's Gorge?" asked Nanny Piggins. She was not sure if it was a geographical feature, or something you found in the pocket of a man who had died from eating too much.

"Dead Man's Gorge is between two cliff faces over-looking a gaping two-hundred-and-nineteen-foot drop into the sea," announced Eduardo melodramatically.

"Oh," said Nanny Piggins, as she mentally tried to picture what two hundred and nineteen feet looked like. A few quick sums gave her the answer—a twenty-story building or, to put it in terms of food (which is how Nanny Piggins always preferred to think of math), two hundred and nineteen foot-long hot dogs laid out end to end.

"Do you accept my challenge, little pig?" asked Eduardo rudely. "Or will you simply surrender any claim you have made for the title of world's greatest flying animal?"

"Let me answer you like this," said Nanny Piggins. And she grabbed the glove, slapped Eduardo hard across the face, and slammed the front door in his snout before he had time to blink. She had yet to prove that she could fly farther than Eduardo, but she certainly had much quicker reflexes than any armadillo.

So Nanny Piggins and the Green children sat with their backs to the front door, thinking (or in Samantha's case, worrying, because that's what she did whenever she thought).

"What are you going to do?" fretted Samantha. She didn't want to see her nanny plummet two hundred and nineteen feet into the sea or, worse still, plummet two hundred and nineteen feet onto the rocks next to the sea.

"You could lay out mattresses on the rocks," suggested Michael.

"You could use a parachute," suggested Derrick.

"You could run away," suggested Samantha.

"It's sweet of you to worry, but there's no need. I'll be fine," said Nanny Piggins warmly. "Beating a flying armadillo shouldn't be too difficult."

"But you can't do it," said Samantha. "You don't have a cannon. And your old circus is miles away. And even if it wasn't, the Ringmaster would never lend you his cannon." (The children had met the Ringmaster, so they knew he was a very wicked man indeed.)

"Piffle," said Nanny Piggins. "Finding a cannon is the easiest thing in the world."

"It is?" asked Derrick, who would not mind having access to a cannon for dealing with Barry Nichols, the school bully.

"Of course," said Nanny Piggins. "They always have them at war museums."

The children could not deny this because there were indeed several large cannons outside the war museum in town.

"But they aren't for people to use," said Samantha.

"Of course they are," argued Nanny Piggins. "Why else would they leave them outside if they didn't want people to borrow them?"

"Um . . ." said Samantha as she tried to think of a better explanation, then realized there wasn't one.

"But if we take a cannon from the war museum, won't the curator think that is very rude?" asked Derrick.

"If you dedicated your life to restoring and displaying military artifacts, would you rather see a cannon stuck outside a museum where grubby children and tourists climb all over it, or at Dead Man's Gorge blasting a pig farther than any pig has ever been blasted before?" asked Nanny Piggins.

The children had to assume that, like them, the curator would want to see the flying pig. So later that day Nanny Piggins and the children caught the bus into town and went to borrow a cannon. They took Boris with them, because if you are planning to move a gigantic cannon, it is handy to have a thousand-pound bear with you to help with the heavy lifting.

There were several cannons to choose from outside the war museum, so Nanny Piggins picked the biggest (her usual policy when choosing anything). Now you might think that security guards, the police, or even just good-hearted bystanders would stop this "borrowing" from taking place in broad daylight. But, as it turned out, the sight of a pig, a bear, and three children taking a cannon from outside the war museum was so strange that no one thought to challenge them.[3]

There was some trouble getting the cannon home. It was a World War I fifteen-inch howitzer and weighed about six tons, so there was no way it was going to fit through the door of the bus. Plus, they were not sure whether the bus driver would give a cannon a ticket. Nanny Piggins thought he should if he allowed baby strollers on the bus. But the children suspected that the bus driver would see strollers and cannons as belonging in two separate categories.

Fortunately the dilemma was solved when Nanny Piggins had a brilliant idea. She got Derrick to distract the bus driver by pretending he had been bitten by a venomous snake. And while he writhed on the floor in pretend pain, Nanny Piggins took the belt off her dress and tied the cannon to the back bumper of the bus. So the cannon was dragged back to Mr. Green's house

---

[3] I must make one thing clear—Nanny Piggins does not encourage theft. She knows stealing is wrong. It is always, always wrong. But borrowing is okay. And as Nanny Piggins always says, if you must borrow something without asking, do it in broad daylight. It gives it a veneer of respectability.

without any problem (although the bus did not get above five miles per hour the whole way).

Back at home, Nanny Piggins, Boris, and the children considered what to do next.

"We've got a cannon," said Derrick. "So is that it? Are you all ready for your duel?"

"Not quite," admitted Nanny Piggins. "I haven't been blasted out of a cannon for months. I'm out of shape."

Boris patted Nanny Piggins comfortingly on the hand. "I didn't want to say anything. But I'm glad you know."

"What shape do you need to be, to be blasted out of a cannon?" asked Michael, thinking of the shapes he had learned about in geometry—squares, circles, and trapezoids.

"That's not what she means," Samantha explained. "When someone says they're 'out of shape,' they mean they haven't been exercising."

"No, Michael's right," said Nanny Piggins. "When I say 'I'm out of shape,' I mean I'm out of shape. My shape's become all lean and skinny. To be a flying pig, I need to be rounder."

"Really?" said Derrick, as he looked at Nanny Piggins. His nanny already ate more than a football team trapped in an elevator for three days with nothing to eat but a packet of breath mints. He could not begin to imagine how much she would consume if she was actually trying to gain weight.

"Oh yes. If I am going to be blasted an enormous distance tomorrow morning, I must immediately start eating," said Nanny Piggins. "You see, it's all to do with physics. You remember what I taught you about Isaac Newton?"

"He was the man who invented gravity," said Michael. "Which is why it hurts if an apple falls on your head."

"Exactly," said Nanny Piggins. "Newton also said that force equals mass times acceleration."

"What does that mean?" asked Derrick.

"It means that if you're fat, you'll fly farther," explained Nanny Piggins.

"Really?" asked Samantha. She did not know much about physics, but she was pretty sure it was more complicated than that.

"Of course I'm sure," said Nanny Piggins.

"Plus the fat helps cushion your landing if you miss your target," added Boris.

"Now quick, Samantha," instructed Nanny Piggins. "You had better call Hans at the bakery."

"What should I tell him to send over?" asked Samantha.

"The truck," said Nanny Piggins, "stocked full of everything from the shop. And tell him to start baking as many cakes as his oven will take. This is an emergency."

And so Hans baked and baked. And Nanny Piggins ate and ate. And the children watched with awed fascination (as they ate a few treats themselves). Perhaps more than all the other things their nanny did brilliantly, Nanny Piggins was phenomenally good at eating. It was a sight to behold. If eating were an Olympic sport, Nanny Piggins would have been the gold medalist every time. Which is probably the only reason they do not have eating at the Olympics, because they do not want the athletes to feel bad about being beaten by a lady pig.

By the time they arrived at Dead Man's Gorge the next morning, Nanny Piggins had certainly managed to get herself "in shape." She looked almost exactly like a huge, round pink bullet. She had never had much of a neck, but what little neck there was had now disappeared entirely.

The children and Boris pushed their borrowed cannon into position next to Eduardo's. Nanny Piggins could not help. She was too busy rolling on the ground groaning, "Urrrgh uggrrr," because of all she had eaten.

"I am surprised you're here," said Eduardo. "I expected you to run away and cower in fear."

"Oh hush up," moaned Nanny Piggins, because for some reason, overeating exhausts the part of the brain that thinks of clever things to say.

"Shall we begin?" asked Eduardo.

"I'm ready when you are," said Nanny Piggins, which actually turned out to be untrue.

For a start, it took a while to get Boris to stop clutching Nanny Piggins to his chest and sobbing, "Please don't do it! It's too dangerous."

Then there was another hitch. Eduardo climbed easily into the barrel of his cannon. After all, he was still working in a circus and was used to being blasted five times a night. Nanny Piggins, however, was out of practice. When she tried to get into her barrel, she soon discovered she had been a little overzealous about "getting into shape."

"You don't fit," worried Samantha.

"Thank goodness. Let's go home!" said Boris.

"Yes I do," argued Nanny Piggins, because she might be out of practice, but she still knew a thing or two about pig ballistics. "Fetch me a big tub of butter."

Fortunately they had a huge tub of butter in Mr. Green's car. Nanny Piggins kept it there for emergencies, such as suddenly coming across hot buns that urgently needed to be eaten.

"Now smear it all over me," ordered Nanny Piggins.

So the children and Boris set to work buttering Nanny Piggins. It took longer than you might expect because Nanny Piggins got peckish and could not resist licking it off. It was not until Michael found a two-year-old expired chocolate bar down the backseat of Mr. Green's car that they were able to distract Nanny Piggins long enough to finish buttering her up.

"Are you sure this is going to work?" asked Derrick.

"Of course I'm sure," said Nanny Piggins. And she was right. Although it did take all her strength and an enormous amount of shoving from all three children and Boris to jam her into the barrel.

"And you call yourself a flying pig," scoffed Eduardo.

"I'll be calling myself *winner* when you eat my dust in a minute," said Nanny Piggins in a muffled voice from deep inside the cannon.

And so the moment of truth arrived. Samantha was going to do the countdown while Derrick and Eduardo's assistant (Sanchez, the Guatemalan guinea pig) stood by, ready to fire the cannons.

It was an anxious moment. Michael clutched Boris's hand. And Derrick tried not to collapse when Boris fell weeping on his shoulder.

"Five, four, three, two, one!" said Samantha as she clamped her eyes shut because she could not bear to look.

Bam!!! went the cannons as they fired loudly, blasting the two animals into the air. Eduardo shot cleanly out of his cannon and made a perfect parabolic arc in the sky. It was a beautiful flight. And very long. Sadly, not quite long enough to get him all the way across

Dead Man's Gorge. He was only six inches short of making the other side. But six inches is a long way when there is a two-hundred-and-nineteen-foot drop below.

"Aaaaaaagggghhhh!!!!!" said Eduardo as he realized he had made a terrible, terrible, terrible mistake.

But, as it turned out, he was lucky. Michael had complete faith in his nanny, but did not have the same amount of faith in the ninety-year-old howitzer or the prevailing headwind she was being blasted into. So he had, unbeknownst to Nanny Piggins, snuck out in the night and put his mattress at the bottom of Dead Man's Gorge. So rest assured, Eduardo did not plummet to his death.

He plummeted to his wet. Because he fell all the way down, hit the mattress, bounced off, and landed in the cold, wintry sea. Which would have been unpleasant for anyone, but was particularly unpleasant for a desert-living armadillo from Mexico who was not used to cold weather.

Now I should tell you what happened to Nanny Piggins. Unfortunately, it is not exactly clear. It turns out (for those of you who do know about physics, you

"Aaaaaaaggggghhhh!!!!!" said Eduardo as he realized he had made a terrible, terrible, terrible mistake.

might be familiar with this) that the tighter you pack the barrel of a cannon, the farther the blast goes. So if you fire a pig that only fits into a cannon with the aid of two gallons of butter, three small children, and a bear, then that pig is going to fly a very long way. Especially if that pig is not particularly good at math and she has particular difficulty with decimal places. So that instead of putting 0.05 pounds of gunpowder into the cannon, Nanny Piggins put 50 pounds of gunpowder into the cannon (for those of you who do not like decimals either, this means she used one thousand times too much).

Simply put, when Nanny Piggins blasted out of the cannon, the children had no idea where she went. All they saw was a streak of pink pig flying across the sky at the speed of light. She passed over Dead Man's Gorge and kept flying until she was a tiny pink dot disappearing over the horizon.

"Uh-oh!" said Derrick.

"Oh no!" said Samantha.

"Cool!" said Michael.

Boris did not say anything because he was too busy whimpering with his paws over his eyes.

Never fear, Nanny Piggins was perfectly all right. She sent the children a telegram later that day to let them know she had landed safely. But they did not see her again for three days because that is how long it took her to walk back.

The first thing Nanny Piggins did upon returning was go to the hospital to see Eduardo. Not that there was anything wrong with him. He was just in the hospital for his nerves. Falling two hundred and nineteen feet into the sea had really shaken him up and totally put him off cannons. So Nanny Piggins had mercy on him. Instead of biting him hard on the leg as she had originally planned, she merely slapped him with a rubber glove that she'd borrowed from one of the nurses, gave him a bag of chocolate chip cookies as a get-well present, and told him to never claim to be the greatest flying anything ever again.

And so Nanny Piggins, Boris, and the children returned home and everything was back to normal. Nanny Piggins had lost her flying "shape" on the three-day walk back, she still held the title of world's greatest flying animal, and the children had the best-ever story for show-and-tell on Monday.

CHAPTER FOUR

Nanny Piggins and the Buzzy Bee Cookies

anny Piggins, Boris, and the children were in Mr. Green's bedroom. For once they were not there to rifle through his drawers looking for spare change, or to "borrow" his clothes to make spaceman costumes. They were in Mr. Green's bedroom because it had the best view of the street. And since it was a rainy day and they could not go outside to harass the community in person, Nanny Piggins suggested that they spend the afternoon blowing spitballs at passing pedestrians who did not look nice. Which, as it turned out, was a delightful way to while away their time.

Nanny Piggins had a point system worked out. You got five points if your spitball hit someone wearing a hat, ten points for a bald man, fifteen points if you got someone in the ear, and twenty points if you got it in the ear of a bald man while he was talking on a cell phone.

The children thoroughly enjoyed the game. Derrick had twenty-five points, Samantha had twenty, and Michael had ten. But Nanny Piggins was easily winning. She had 1,695 points. Although admittedly she had an advantage. While she was touring with the circus, Nanny Piggins had met a South American pygmy who taught her how to use a dart gun with startling power and accuracy. She could hit a mosquito in midair from five hundred feet away. And, of course, it helped that she had Boris dangling her out the window by her hind legs, allowing her to get as close as possible to her target.

Nanny Piggins was just about to hit a bald man in the ear as he talked on a cell phone while picking his nose at the same time when she spotted a girl walking along the street.

"Pull me in! Quick!! It's the police," squealed Nanny

Piggins, which nearly caused Boris to drop her. He did not like being yelled at, even when the yelling was meant in the friendliest possible way. He had delicate nerves for a bear.

Derrick, Samantha, and Michael leaned farther out the window to see what Nanny Piggins was talking about.

"It's just a girl," said Derrick.

"Yes, but she's wearing a blue police uniform," countered Nanny Piggins.

"I think she's too short to be in the police force," suggested Michael.

"Perhaps she's wearing a disguise," said Nanny Piggins, "and secretly she's six foot two."

"Or," said Samantha, "perhaps she's a Buzzy Bee. They wear blue uniforms too."

"A what-what?" asked Nanny Piggins.

"A Buzzy Bee," explained Samantha.

"What are they?" asked Nanny Piggins.

This stumped Samantha for a moment. She was not entirely sure how best to explain it. "It's an organization for girls...where they learn how to do good deeds for the community...and how to survive in the wilderness...and they go camping."

"Camping!" exclaimed Nanny Piggins. "The poor creatures. How inhumanely cruel. What sort of wicked adults would condone taking children out into the wilderness and depriving them of toilet facilities?"

"It's supposed to do them good," explained Derrick.

"Typical!" said Nanny Piggins. "Humans never cease to amaze me. I still can't get over how giving children an oval ball and letting them run at full tilt, slamming into each other, is legal." She did not at all approve of organized sports. Disorganized sports like pie throwing, ice-cream-van chasing, and being shot out of a cannon held much more appeal.

"Look!" cried Boris. "She's coming this way! Quick, hide!"

The blond girl was, indeed, letting herself in through the Greens' front gate and approaching the front door. Unfortunately there was no time to avoid detection, because a ten-foot squealing Russian bear does tend to draw the eye.

The girl smiled and waved up at them.

Nanny Piggins and the children stared back down. (Boris was too busy "hiding." Although he was not so much hiding as cowering in the corner with

Mr. Green's quilt over his head. But we should not judge him too harshly because it is hard to hide when you are ten feet tall and weigh over a thousand pounds.)

"What does she want?" hissed Nanny Piggins. She distrusted unprovoked smiling. It was the type of thing dentists do right before they start drilling into your teeth. So she clutched her dart gun tightly and wished she had not left the poisoned darts in her own room.

"We could go downstairs and ask her," suggested Samantha, knowing this was something Nanny Piggins would never think of herself.

"All right," said Nanny Piggins. "But if we are all arrested and dragged off to prison, it'll be your fault when we miss our soap operas."

So they all went downstairs (except for Boris, who was still hiding under the quilt) and approached the front door with caution. Nanny Piggins was holding a retractable umbrella at the ready, just in case things got out of hand and someone had to be clubbed over the head.

"If I am arrested, children," said Nanny Piggins, "I just want you to know two things. One, it's been a pleasure being your nanny. And two, I've got twenty-three fun-size packets of mini chocolate bars sewn into the underside of my mattress. I want you to eat them and think of all the wonderful times we've had together."

And with that Nanny Piggins bravely swung open the front door.

"Good morning," said the girl. "Would you like to buy some Buzzy Bee cookies?"

Nanny Piggins immediately slammed the door in her face.

"What does she mean?" Nanny Piggins asked the children.

"I think she'd like to know if you'd like to buy some Buzzy Bee cookies," said Derrick. (He realized it took his nanny no time at all to grasp things that made no sense, and a lot of time to understand things that seemed perfectly reasonable.)

"But that's the most stupid question in the entire world," said Nanny Piggins.

"It is?" said Samantha. This surprised her because only the previous day, her math teacher had told her that the stupidest question in the entire world was "Why do I have to learn how to solve quadratic equations?"

"Who would *not* want to buy cookies?" asked

Nanny Piggins. "It's like asking, 'Would you like to breathe in and out?' or 'Would you like to try to shove twenty-three fun-size packets of chocolate into your mouth all at the same time?' The answer is obvious." And with that Nanny Piggins threw the door back open and told the now slightly frightened-looking girl, "Yes, of course I want to buy your cookies. What a ridiculous question! How can the answer be anything other than—yes, yes, yes!!!"

As it turned out, Nanny Piggins only bought nine boxes of cookies. She would have bought more, but the problem was she was paid ten cents an hour and Nanny Piggins had only found eleven dollars when she was looking for a dropped M&M under the floor mats in Mr. Green's car.

So Nanny Piggins, the children, and Boris (who had now been convinced that it was safe to come downstairs) sat with the packets of cookies laid out on the coffee table ready to enjoy a lovely afternoon tea. Nanny Piggins opened the first packet, handed them around to the others, and then took one for herself.

Eating the first cookie out of a fresh packet was a serious ritual for Nanny Piggins. First, she held the cookie to her nose. It smelled good—buttery and sweet. Next, she held the cookie to the light to inspect the color—a perfect golden brown. And finally, she held the cookie to her mouth and shoved in the whole thing, in one gulp.

Normally at this point she would moan with pleasure. But not this time.

"Noooooo!" screamed Nanny Piggins, cookie crumbs flying out from her mouth in all directions. She then leaped up and threw over the coffee table, scattering the cookies all over the floor.

"What's wrong?" asked Derrick.

"Don't eat another bite!" exclaimed Nanny Piggins.

"Why?" asked Samantha, starting to feel worried because she had just swallowed a large bite.

"Are they poisoned?" asked Boris.

"Are they disgusting?" asked Michael.

"Do you want them all to yourself?" asked Samantha.

"No. Much, much worse than all that. They're stolen!" proclaimed Nanny Piggins.

The others stared at Nanny Piggins in horror.

"How can you tell?" asked Derrick.

"Taste them!" said Nanny Piggins.

"I thought you didn't want us to have another bite?" said Michael, who wanted a bite but did not want his nanny to scold him.

"You can have just one bite," conceded Nanny Piggins.

The children each took a bite of their cookies. It tasted like cookie to them. Very good cookie, but cookie nonetheless. But then they did not know what stolen property tasted like.

It was Boris who recognized it instantly. As soon as the first cookie crumbs touched his taste buds, he was spitting them back out across the room and screaming, "You're right! Definitely stolen!"

"You see," said Nanny Piggins, who enjoyed being correct.

"So you're saying that girl broke into someone's house and stole all these cookies?" asked Derrick. (He did not realize his nanny had such a good sense of taste.)

"No, I'm saying she stole them from my family," said Nanny Piggins.

Now the children were really confused.

"These are my great-great-grandmother's cookies," explained Nanny Piggins.

"But surely they'd be past their use-by date," said Michael as he read the back of one of the boxes.

"No, I mean it is my great-great-grandmother's recipe," said Nanny Piggins.

"Oh," said the children as they finally started to catch on.

"But are you absolutely sure?" asked Derrick. "I mean, cookies all taste much the same."

Nanny Piggins gripped the sofa and stared at Derrick in horror. "Derrick," said Nanny Piggins. "How could you say such ugly words?!"

"Sorry," said Derrick, realizing he had just said something terribly offensive.

Boris patted Nanny Piggins's hand soothingly as she struggled to contain her emotions. "Every cookie in the world is unique," Boris explained to the children. "The ratio of sugar to flour to butter to nutmeg—it's as unique as DNA in humans."

"More unique!" declared Nanny Piggins. "No one has ever adequately explained to me how identical twins work."

"True," said Boris, nodding.

"There is no doubt about it," said Nanny Piggins,

sniffing another cookie. "This is Great-Great-Granny Piggins's cookie. How else could it be so delicious?"

And so, while Nanny Piggins, Boris, and the children thoroughly checked all the cookies (by eating them), she came up with a plan. "I need to infiltrate the Buzzy Bees," decided Nanny Piggins.

"Couldn't you just report them to the police?" suggested Samantha reasonably.

"This is too serious a matter for the police," said Nanny Piggins unreasonably. "It's not enough to just lock them up in jail forever and ever. We need to find out how they stole the recipe. Then punish them *properly*."

"Why?" asked Derrick, who thought that sounded like an awful lot of work.

"Because if they got the cookie recipe, who knows what they might try to steal next?" exclaimed Nanny Piggins. "Seventh-Cousin Gillian's peanut brittle? Third-Niece Natalie's blancmange? Or worst of all — what if Great-Great-Auntie Piggins's chocolate mud cake recipe got out?!!" Nanny Piggins had to stop speaking here because she got so emotional she could not say another word.

Boris patted her affectionately on the shoulder.

"There, there. Don't think about it. The possibilities are too horrific to imagine."

"So how does one go about joining the Buzzy Bees?" asked Nanny Piggins, pulling herself together. "Is there an initiation ritual? Do I have to kidnap a goat? Or ride a motorbike through a burning ring of fire?"

"I'm pretty sure you just have to go along to one of their meetings and say you'd like to join," said Samantha.

"Of course, how ingenious, they make it easy so they can lure more young people into a life of crime," said Nanny Piggins, nodding wisely. "Let's all go and join tomorrow."

As it turned out they did not all go and join the Buzzy Bees the next day. Derrick and Michael, after an enormous amount of explanation and begging, managed to excuse themselves. Nanny Piggins took some time to be convinced that the Buzzy Bees was only for girls. She was pretty sure this must breach some equal-opportunity law or another.

But in the end it was just Nanny Piggins, Samantha,

and Boris (who was a ballet dancer and therefore in touch with his feminine side, and did not mind pretending to be an eleven-year-old girl) who went along to the Buzzy Bee meeting.

When they arrived, the blond girl who had sold them the cookies was also there. Although as soon as she saw Nanny Piggins, she ran away screaming. The adult leader of the group, a stout, jolly, middle-aged woman, came up to welcome them.

"Hello, I'm Barn Owl," she said.

"She does realize she's not an owl, she's a human, doesn't she?" Nanny Piggins whispered to Samantha.

"I think so," said Samantha, who was entirely out of her depth.

"Maybe she calls herself Barn Owl because her head will turn around three hundred and sixty degrees," suggested Boris.

"Good point," said Nanny Piggins. "Shall we find out?"

"Maybe later," suggested Samantha, grabbing Nanny Piggins's trotter. Samantha thought that twisting the leader's neck was probably not a good way to make friends and feel part of the group.

"She does realize she's not an owl, she's a human, doesn't she?" Nanny Piggins whispered to Samantha.

"Why don't our new members stand up and introduce themselves?" said Barn Owl.

"Hello," said Nanny Piggins. "I'm Na—Sarah."

"I'm Samantha," said Samantha.

"And I'm Borisina," said Boris in a high-pitched, feminine voice.

"All right, it's jolly good to have some new girls. Let's make them feel welcome the Buzzy Bee way," said Barn Owl.

Nanny Piggins turned to Samantha. "Is this where they make us jump a motorbike through a burning ring of fire?"

But, sadly, Nanny Piggins was disappointed.

"Let's take them outside and teach them how to light a fire with just two sticks," said Barn Owl.

The next two hours were not terribly instructive for Nanny Piggins, Boris, and Samantha. Watching girls rub two sticks together without generating even a puff of smoke was not Nanny Piggins's idea of a good time.

"They do realize you can buy a box of matches for twenty cents, don't they?" asked Nanny Piggins.

"I think they want to be able to light a fire when they find themselves somewhere without shops that sell matches," explained Samantha.

"Surely it would be a thousand times easier just to carry a box of matches at all times," said Boris.

"I suppose they want to know how to light a fire if they fall in a river and their matches get wet," said Samantha.

"If this is the alternative, I'd rather stay in the river and be swept out to sea," said Nanny Piggins. (She did not really mean this. But watching the girls rubbing sticks together was making her very bored.)

"Should I run down to the service station and get them some gasoline to help start their fires?" suggested Boris, because he was a very kind and helpful bear.

"I think they're meant to be able to do it without gasoline," said Samantha.

"At this rate, the only way they are going to start a fire is if one of them gets struck by lightning," said Nanny Piggins, looking at her watch.

"I don't think that's very likely," said Boris sadly, looking up at the sky. "There aren't any clouds around."

"All right, that's enough of fire lighting," said Barn Owl. "You've all done jolly well. Melinda's sticks are really quite warm. I'm sure we'll have a roaring fire when we try again next week. Now let's go inside and play games."

"Ooh, games! I like games!" said Nanny Piggins. "I do hope we play something good, like Laser Tag or Lava Floor."

Sadly Nanny Piggins was, yet again, disappointed. Barn Owl's idea of "a jolly game" involved breaking up into teams and seeing who was fastest at passing a beanbag from one end of the room to the other.

"I don't see the point of this game at all," said Nanny Piggins as she flung her beanbag to Boris with the speed and accuracy of a Major League Baseball pitcher. "No one ever needs a beanbag with any degree of urgency. It's totally pointless. It's not helping us find the thief at—"

Nanny Piggins froze mid-rant because she had just spotted something shocking on the wall.

"Aaaaggghhh!" said Nanny Piggins.

"What's wrong?" asked Samantha.

"It's not a wasp, is it?" said Boris as he curled himself into a ball on the floor.

"That woman!!!" said Nanny Piggins.

"What woman?" asked Samantha.

Nanny Piggins was temporarily at a loss for words, so she just pointed. Samantha and Boris looked in the direction of Nanny Piggins's outstretched trotter. And sure enough, there on the wall was an enlarged black-and-white photograph of a stern-looking old woman.

"I knew an evil mastermind had to be behind the cookie theft, but I never could have imagined it was her!" declared Nanny Piggins.

"Who is it?" asked Samantha.

"That is our beloved patron, the founder of the Buzzy Bees—Lady Marigold Pickford," said Barn Owl, who had just joined them and was now smiling fondly at the photograph.

As Barn Owl drifted away to oversee the beanbag race in another part of the room, Nanny Piggins huddled together with Samantha and Boris. "She founded the Buzzy Bees?! I didn't know her wickedness extended that far!"

"But how do you know Lady Marigold Pickford?" asked Samantha, burning with curiosity.

"Great-Great-Granny Piggins looked after Lady Marigold Pickford's children. She was their nanny," said Nanny Piggins.

"No way!" said Boris. "Get out! That's, like, totally surprising." (Boris was getting very good at pretending to be a young girl.)

"Lady Marigold Pickford was unspeakably cruel," continued Nanny Piggins. "She would force her children to get out of bed at six AM."

"No!" gasped Samantha.

"Every morning!" continued Nanny Piggins. "And that's not all. She forced them to do physical exercise."

Now Samantha and Boris both gasped.

"Even when it was raining?" asked Boris.

"Even when there was something good on TV?" asked Samantha.

"Even if it was raining *and* there was something good on television," said Nanny Piggins.

"The witch!" cried Boris.

"Lady Marigold Pickford must have stolen Great-Great-Granny Piggins's cookie recipe while Great-

Great-Granny was working for her," said Nanny Piggins.

"Was she really that wicked?" asked Samantha.

"Oh yes," said Nanny Piggins. "Great-Great-Granny Piggins would often collapse from exhaustion because Lady Marigold Pickford would allow no cake in the house."

Samantha gasped. She knew what this meant to a pig.

"If she could force children to exercise on a rainy day, then she was capable of anything," said Boris.

"So does that mean we can go home and stop pretending to be Buzzy Bees?" asked Samantha. "Lady Marigold Pickford has been dead for years and years, so there's nothing we can do about the stolen recipe now."

"Nothing we can do?!" said Nanny Piggins disbelievingly. "If we are going to fight this injustice, there are a million things we can do!"

"There are?" asked Samantha, starting to worry.

"First of all, we have to get revenge," said Nanny Piggins.

"Of course," said Boris, because he was Russian and revenge was big in Russia.

"But it's only a cookie recipe," said Samantha. "Wouldn't it be easier to forget about it?"

"Forget about it?!" exclaimed Nanny Piggins, then, quickly struggling to control herself, continued. "Sorry, I don't mean to yell. I know it's not your fault. It's the way you're raised. Humans have no principles. But I am a pig. I have my family honor to maintain. It is my duty to exact revenge."

"But how?" asked Samantha.

"Just watch," said Nanny Piggins darkly as she climbed up on a chair and addressed the whole group. "Attention, everybody. I have decided to destroy the Buzzy Bees by starting my own rival organization— the Pig Scouts!"

And that is exactly what she did. As it turned out, the Pig Scouts was actually a brilliant idea. In a few short weeks they became much more popular than the Buzzy Bees. Because, as the large Pig Scout posters Nanny Piggins stuck up all over town made clear, the Pig Scouts had a much more sensible philosophy. The

Buzzy Bees were always taught to "be prepared," but Nanny Piggins taught the Pig Scouts to "be *un*prepared." Because being unprepared made life much more interesting.

While the Buzzy Bees taught girls how to light fires, the Pig Scouts learned to put out fires, which, as Nanny Piggins said, "is a much more important skill. Anyone can light a fire. I do it all the time, sometimes without even realizing, whereas putting a fire out can be quite hard work."

The Buzzy Bees earned badges for "Needlepoint," "Orienteering," and "Turkey Calling." All completely useless skills according to Nanny Piggins. So the Pig Scouts earned badges for really important things like "Eating," "More Eating," and "Digestion." And most importantly, Pig Scouts were taught to keep these badges in a drawer. And never *ever* sew them on their clothes, because it would only ruin a designer outfit.

The uniform of the Pig Scouts was much better than the Buzzy Bee uniform. "Our uniform is to wear no uniform," said Nanny Piggins at their first meeting. "Everyone has to dress differently. In fact, if any two girls turn up to Pig Scouts wearing the same clothes, they will be immediately sent home to change." This did tend to delay the start of meetings quite a lot, but it was worth it because everybody looked fabulous.

Instead of "Dollar-for-Deeds" week, when Buzzy Bees asked friends and neighbors for money in exchange for doing household chores, the Pig Scouts had "Dollar-for-No-Deeds," when they got people to pay them for *not* doing household chores. This was an enormous success. It turns out most people would much rather not have their car washed, floor swept, or lawn raked by a small child who has no idea what they are doing.

But most importantly of all, the Pig Scouts planned their own cookie drive. And in her bid to totally cripple the Buzzy Bees, Nanny Piggins came up with a master stroke. She took her great-great-granny's cookie recipe and made it even more delicious (by adding chocolate chips). Nanny Piggins knew that once the Pig Scout cookies went on sale, no one would ever want to buy a Buzzy Bee cookie again.

So by the end of the month, Nanny Piggins had brought all the local Buzzy Bee units to their knees. The only girls turning up to meetings were the ones related to the leaders and one eight-year-old who was frightened of Nanny Piggins because she yelled at her for eating a bacon sandwich.

Nanny Piggins's scheme of revenge came to its glorious conclusion when Barn Owl turned up at Mr. Green's doorstep in tears.

"Do come in," said Nanny Piggins. She could be gracious now that she had won.

Barn Owl went into the living room and collapsed in a chair, sobbing. "Please, please, you have to stop this. If the Pig Scouts spread out nationally, then internationally, the Buzzy Bees will be finished."

"Exactly," said Nanny Piggins.

"But why would you set out to destroy an organization that only strives to do good works in the community and provide healthy outdoor activities for young girls?" asked Barn Owl as Samantha handed her a fresh tissue so she could weep some more.

"Because there are some things much more important than good deeds and healthy children," said Nanny Piggins. "Such as my family's sacred cookie recipe being stolen by the Buzzy Bees!"

"The cookie recipe!" exclaimed Barn Owl. "It comes from your family?"

"Of course! No one but a Piggins could devise a cookie that delicious," said Boris. He was proud of his sister.

"Then the legend is true," said Barn Owl, a look of awe upon her face.

"What legend?" asked Derrick.

"According to Buzzy Bee lore, a great pig with super culinary powers gave the cookie recipe to Lady Marigold Pickford shortly after the Buzzy Bees was founded," explained Barn Owl.

"Hah," scoffed Nanny Piggins. "Why on earth would my great-great-grandmother share a cookie recipe with someone as unworthy as a non-pig?"

"Apparently she did it to get Lady Marigold Pickford to hush up," said Barn Owl. "I believe she could be a bit of a nag."

"That makes sense," conceded Nanny Piggins. "The Pigginses have always used food as a way of silencing people. It is also good for drawing people out, getting people to reveal secrets, and persuading people to spontaneously do cartwheels."

"So can we call a truce?" begged Barn Owl.

"Better than that," said Nanny Piggins. "I will entirely disband the Pig Scouts."

"Why?" exclaimed Samantha. "Things are going so well."

"Because I don't believe in organizations," explained Nanny Piggins. "They're fine when you need to get revenge for your family's stolen cookie recipe. But girls don't need an organization to teach them how to be girls. Girls are much better off figuring out how to be girls for themselves."

"I couldn't agree with you less," said Barn Owl.

"I know," said Nanny Piggins. "But I wouldn't dream of crushing you just for being wrong. Only if you try to steal my family's cookie recipe."

"Thank you," said Barn Owl.

"Have a cookie," offered Nanny Piggins (the greatest conciliatory gesture a pig can offer).

So Barn Owl left a happy Buzzy Bee leader. And Nanny Piggins disbanded the Pig Scouts before their cookie drive had even begun. So she, Boris, and the children were able to spend a happy week eating their way through two hundred cases of delicious chocolate chip cookies.

CHAPTER FIVE

Nanny Piggins and the Personal Advertisement

"Nanny Piggins! Nanny Piggins!!" shrieked Michael.

"What is it?" asked Nanny Piggins, which just goes to show what a caring nanny she was, because Nanny Piggins was watching her favorite soap opera, *The Young and the Irritable*, with Derrick, Samantha, and Boris. And normally if anyone tried to speak to Nanny Piggins while Bethany was telling Bridge that their son was really his brother's nephew's father, Nanny Piggins would have pretended she was deaf until the commercial break. But Nanny Piggins could tell from the note of horror in Michael's voice that something serious was going on (not as serious as Bethany's twin sister coming out of a coma on *The Young and the Irritable*, but still pretty serious).

"I found this," gasped Michael as he waved a crumpled-up scrap of paper.

"Found it? You haven't been climbing into Dumpsters again, have you? What have I told you about that?" demanded Nanny Piggins.

"I must never climb into Dumpsters without you," chanted Michael, "because it's not fair to let you miss out on all the fun."

"Exactly," said Nanny Piggins approvingly.

"But I didn't find this in a Dumpster," said Michael. "I found it in the bin in Father's office."

"You were searching your father's rubbish bin?" exclaimed Nanny Piggins. "Why? We only searched it yesterday."

"No, I wasn't searching," explained Michael. "I was just looking for something unimportant to spit my gum into, like his checkbook, when I found this."

Nanny Piggins looked more closely at the crumpled

piece of paper. She smoothed it out on her thigh. It was a handwritten note, with lots of crossings out and corrections, written by Mr. Green.

It read: *Wealthy attractive lawyer who drives a Rolls-Royce seeks wife to clean house and look after children. Applicants must not pester me with problems, concerns, or any type of conversation.*

"What is this?" asked Nanny Piggins.

"It's a personal ad," said Derrick.

"A personal what?" asked Nanny Piggins.

"Advertisement," said Derrick. "If you're lonely and you want to meet someone, you can put an advertisement in the newspaper saying what type of person you're looking for, and if anyone is interested, they write back."

"But that's ridiculous. There are people everywhere. The streets are full of them. If Mr. Green wanted to meet someone, he could just walk out his front door," said Nanny Piggins.

"I don't think Father wants to meet someone," said Samantha. "He just wants to get married. If he could do that without ever meeting the woman, I'm sure he would."

"It's all very well for him to get a wife from the sad, lonely women who read newspapers," said Nanny Piggins, "but that is no way to find you a mother."

"I don't know what we can do about it," said Derrick.

"Fetch me the bus timetable!" said Nanny Piggins. "Maybe there's time to go into town and burn down the newspaper office before they print their next edition."

"We can't do that," said Samantha.

"Why not?" asked Nanny Piggins.

"*The Bold and the Spiteful* is on in five minutes," said Samantha.

"Good point," said Nanny Piggins. (*The Bold and the Spiteful* was Nanny Piggins's second-favorite soap opera. She was not going to miss it just to burn down a newspaper office.)

"We will have to come up with another solution," said Nanny Piggins.

"We could always do nothing," suggested Boris. Bears were very good at doing nothing. They did absolutely nothing for four months every winter when they hibernated. This took a lot of willpower and an awful lot of hard-drive space on his TiVo because he didn't like missing *The Bold and the Spiteful* either.

"Hmm...nothing, I like that idea," mused Nanny Piggins. The commercial break was coming to an end and she secretly wanted to keep watching her soap opera.

"After all, Mr. Green can place an advertisement," said Boris. "But no one in her right mind would want to marry him once she'd met him."

"Excellent point!" exclaimed Nanny Piggins. "And terminally silly people wouldn't read newspapers, would they?"

"No," agreed the children.

"And who else would apply?" concluded Nanny Piggins.

No one seemed the obvious answer. So Nanny Piggins, Boris, and the children went back to watching their program.

Unfortunately, Boris's plan to do nothing did not work. Mr. Green was inundated with replies. Every day, the mailbox was filled with perfume-drenched letters. Many with pink or lilac stationery and some even sealed with a lipstick kiss.

On the bright side, however, Mr. Green was too oblivious to think of monitoring his mail. So Nanny Piggins, Boris, and the children were able to have a lovely time every afternoon, steaming open the envelopes and reading all the letters. Of course, they were not able to read *all* the letters. Some were not written in English. Some were written in English but did not make any sense. And one was entirely written in marmalade, so it soon became illegible because Boris could not resist licking it.

"These letters are disgusting," said Nanny Piggins after reading the fiftieth putrid love poem admiring Mr. Green's wealth and Rolls-Royce. "We had better destroy them all."

"Isn't that a little unfair to Father?" suggested Samantha. "Maybe he is lonely and it would be nice for him to get remarried."

Nanny Piggins, Derrick, Michael, and Boris stared at Samantha for a moment. No one knew quite what to say. "You have met your father, haven't you?" asked

Nanny Piggins kindly. "Do you honestly think getting married would make him happy?"

"I suppose not," said Samantha. Mr. Green did have a knack for finding the gloomy side of everything.

The problem was that Samantha read a lot of romance novels, so on some level she secretly hoped that her father had just been pretending to be mean and uncaring for the last nine years and that secretly he was nice and normal.

"Just because these women are clearly deluded and deranged," continued Nanny Piggins, "does not mean they deserve to be exposed to your father. I suggest we burn all the letters and bury the ashes in a deep hole down at the far end of the garden."

And that is exactly what they did. The letters made quite a merry fire once Nanny Piggins poured some kerosene on them. And the children were able to toast marshmallows over the embers of their father's romantic aspirations.[4]

Unfortunately Nanny Piggins had underestimated

---

[4] Dear Reader, I am not allowed to mention fire without reminding you that you must never *ever* light a fire yourself, unless under the close supervision of a responsible adult pig with advanced circus training.

just how much some single women want to get married. It never occurred to her that one of them would have the audacity to actually come to the house. And so the next day when the doorbell rang, Nanny Piggins wishfully assumed it was a lost pizza-delivery boy who was going to give them free prepaid pizzas. She flung the door open, only to be confronted by a woman standing right there on their doorstep. The words "Yummy! Give me the pizzas..." died on Nanny Piggins's lips.

One look at the beautiful petite brunette with her peaches-and-cream complexion and sparkling brown eyes (magnified alluringly by horn-rimmed glasses), and Nanny Piggins knew she was in trouble.

"Hello, I'm here about Mr. Green's personal advertisement," said the Mrs. Green–want-to-be.

"Go away!" screamed Nanny Piggins as she immediately tried to slam the door.

But this woman, like Nanny Piggins, had surprising strength for her diminutive stature. As soon as Nanny Piggins moved to slam the door, she jammed her shoulder into it, and a pushing match ensued. Nanny Piggins and the Mrs. Green–want-to-be both pushed as hard as they could. But the door never wavered more than a millimeter in either direction.

"Go away," grunted Nanny Piggins.

"Let me in," wheezed the Mrs. Green–want-to-be.

The children rushed out into the hallway to see what their nanny was doing.

"Can we help?" asked Derrick.

"Whatever you do, don't let your father see her," panted Nanny Piggins.

Mr. Green was practically never home. He spent as much time as he possibly could at work, preferably on business trips, so he could avoid his children as much as possible. To find Mr. Green at home was actually incredibly difficult. You would have to watch the house like a hawk to know that he was there. So either the Mrs. Green–want-to-be was incredibly lucky or she had been hiding in the bushes across the street with a pair of field binoculars for four days.

When Mr. Green was home, he had one rule. "Children must be neither seen nor heard nor smelled, and definitely not touched." He had this laminated onto note cards and given to each of the children. If Derrick, Samantha, or Michael was ever caught breaking this rule, he got very annoyed. (You could tell because his neck turned red. He never actually told the children he was annoyed, because that would involve making eye contact, and he tried to avoid that.)

So when Mr. Green burst into the corridor and said with a slightly raised voice, "What is all this ruckus!?" they knew he was really mad.

The children instinctively tried to hide—Derrick behind the umbrella stand, Samantha under a pile of raincoats, and Michael in the hall closet. Which left Nanny Piggins momentarily distracted, because Derrick had accidentally jabbed her in the eye with an umbrella. The Mrs. Green–want-to-be used this opportunity to give one enormous shove, pushing Nanny Piggins and the front door aside and making her entrance into the Green home.

"Mr. Green?" said the Mrs. Green–want-to-be. "My name is Jane Doeadear. I have come about your personal advertisement."

Mr. Green did not so much respond as slobber and bounce about, much like a happy puppy. When he placed the advertisement, Mr. Green had simply wanted a free housekeeper/nanny/domestic slave so he could rid himself of the shame of having a pig for a nanny. He had very low standards. He was prepared to marry any woman willing to scrub the baked-on scum off his oven. It never occurred to him (or to be fair, anybody else) that he could find a wife who was also dazzlingly attractive. And Jane Doeadear definitely was that. She was just the type of woman Mr. Green liked—beautiful, shiny-haired, and with glasses (he rightly thought that women with poor eyesight were more likely to find him attractive, or at least less likely to find him unattractive).

Even Nanny Piggins had to admit that this stranger was good-looking. She had a sort of jaunty athleticism that Nanny Piggins found oddly familiar. It was almost as if they had met before, but Nanny Piggins could not remember where.

"Hello," said Mr. Green in such a way that he clearly thought he was being dazzlingly attractive himself. He sort of smirked, winked, and tried to look thin all at once. Fortunately the children could not see because they were trying to hide. But Nanny Piggins saw and it almost made her violently ill (which would have been a terrible tragedy because she had eaten the most delicious blueberry pancakes for breakfast—Nanny Piggins's secret for making really good blueberry pancakes was to use chocolate chips instead of blueberries).

"Do come in," simpered Mr. Green.

And that is how Jane Doeadear invaded the Green family home. Mr. Green immediately invited her to stay in the guest room. He thought it would be cheaper than dating. And it would give him an opportunity to observe Jane's cleaning abilities up close.

The next week was a horrible one for Nanny Piggins and the children. Mr. Green started coming home from work at a normal time, just so he could watch Jane doing housework and sigh blissfully.

"Do you think Father is suffering from some sort of brain damage?" asked Michael.

"Yes," said Nanny Piggins as they watched him watching Jane. "But it's no more severe than usual. Attractive women always have this effect on men."

"It's almost as if he's been hit on the head with a baseball bat," observed Samantha.

"It's worse than that," said Nanny Piggins. "When you hit someone on the head with a baseball bat, the sharp pain and swollen bruise let them know something is wrong. But when a man is dazzled by a beautiful woman, he doesn't realize he has gone temporarily insane. The opposite happens. He suddenly thinks he is the funniest, cleverest man ever to walk the earth. Really, when single men start dating, they should all be locked up in lunatic asylums."

"How are we going to get rid of her?" asked Derrick.

"Are you sure you want to?" asked Nanny Piggins.

"What?!" exclaimed all three Green children. "Of course we want to get rid of her."

"But you haven't gotten to know her yet. And she has done a lovely job of cleaning the oven, sweeping the patio, and disinfecting the Tupperware. Wouldn't you like to have a new mother?" asked Nanny Piggins. Much as she loved the children herself, she knew it would be selfish to obstruct them from having a new mother, if that was what they wanted.

The Green children had to think about this for a moment.

"I still like our old mother," said Michael, sniffing.

The three Green children thought about their own mother, who actually used to talk to them, bake them cakes, and kiss them good night when she tucked them in. Their eyes became wet and itchy.

"I know no one can replace your own mother," said Nanny Piggins kindly, "but this woman might grow on you." Nanny Piggins knew that Jane was unpleasant and emotionally distant. But there was something familiar about Jane Doeadear that made Nanny Piggins feel a kinship with her.

They watched as she polished the silver teapot so hard the sun glinted off it and blinded them.

"I doubt it," said Samantha.

"There's something else..." Derrick struggled to put his finger on what it was that was wrong with Jane Doeadear.

"Clean!" said Michael. "She's just too clean."

And Nanny Piggins had to admit that Jane had done a thorough job of demolishing the bacteria population of the Green house.

Sadly, Mr. Green did not share his children's concerns. He loved being able to see his face in the side of the kettle, the tops of his shoes, and the bathroom mirror. He was delighted with the hygiene improvements Jane had made in a few short days. Since Nanny Piggins had been living in the house, he had become used to seeing chocolate and honey smeared on just about everything.

Jane Doeadear had only been staying for one week when, at breakfast, Mr. Green cleared his throat and said, "I have an announcement to make." He looked around and smiled at his children, which only made them fear the worst. He had not smiled at them since he had announced he would stop giving them pocket money. Mr. Green cleared his throat again for dramatic effect. "I have asked Jane to marry me."

"And what did Jane say?" asked Nanny Piggins, barely able to conceal her astonishment.

"Yes," said Jane before returning her attention to her eggs and hash browns.

"We're getting married on Saturday," said Mr. Green. "I'm taking the morning off work for the ceremony," he added, smiling fondly at his fiancée, who was ignoring him. Just what he wanted in a wife.

The children were too astonished to speak. Mr.

Green stood up to leave. "So, er, Miss Piggins"—it was always a bad sign when he stopped calling Nanny Piggins *Nanny*—"we won't be needing your services anymore. I'm giving you two weeks' notice."

Derrick lunged at his father. He would have strangled him too if the serving dish Samantha threw at Mr. Green had not hit Derrick in the head instead. Michael had gone for a more pacifist approach. He had merely barred the door and yelled, "Noooo, we won't let you!"

But Mr. Green did not hear his son; he was too blissfully in love with his own cleverness. Marrying a woman was going to cost practically nothing, whereas paying Nanny Piggins cost slightly more than nothing.

"I have to go to work. Darling," Mr. Green said, turning to Jane, "could you take my car in to the garage for me? The engine is making a funny noise."

"Certainly, darling," said Jane. "But there's no need to pay a mechanic. I can take a look at it. I know a thing or two about motorcars."

"A fiancée who cleans *and* does automotive repairs!" gushed Mr. Green as he imagined the fortune he was going to save on getting his car serviced. "I am such a clever...I mean, lucky, man."

Mr. Green handed his fiancée the keys to the car and left.

Nanny Piggins and the children turned their attention to Jane. She was still calmly eating her breakfast.

"Do you have a history of mental illness in your family?" enquired Nanny Piggins.

"You can't honestly want to marry Father!" said Derrick.

"I'll give you my teddy bear if you just go away," said Michael.

Jane finished her mouthful and looked up. "Just because I'm marrying your father does not mean I have to speak to any of you. Once the marriage certificate is signed, I don't plan to speak to him either. Now kindly stand aside. I have to see to your father's car." With that, she left.

"There is nothing for it, children. I can't allow you to be left in this woman's care," said Nanny Piggins. "We shall have to get rid of her."

"But how?" asked Derrick.

"With stealth and intelligence," said Nanny Piggins. "Or brute force. Whichever works best."

So Nanny Piggins and the children set about trying to discredit their future stepmother. (Fortunately, they had plenty of opportunity because Jane spent all day locked in the garage, like a good future wife, working on Mr. Green's car.) They searched her room but found nothing incriminating. All she had was a suitcase full of lovely designer dresses, and a one-hundred-and-eight-piece wrench set, which was odd but not illegal.

Next, Nanny Piggins tried using brute force. She told Jane there was a nickel under the sofa, and when Jane lay down on the floor to look for it, Nanny Piggins rolled her up in the Persian carpet, put the carpet in the wheelbarrow, and had Boris wheel her down to the garbage dump. But, sadly, it did not work. Jane always carried a pocketknife, so she was able to cut her way out of the carpet, jump up, and bop Boris over the head, then walk back to the house again.

The children even tried having her locked up. Working on the assumption that anyone who wanted to marry their father must be criminally insane, they went down to the police station and tried to have her institutionalized. But, surprisingly, there were no outstanding arrest warrants for Jane Doeadear. She had not escaped from any local mental institutions. She did not even have a criminal record.

So the morning of the wedding arrived and the children were very sad indeed. Once the ceremony and the reception (a cup of tea out of a thermos on the courthouse steps) were over, they would have a new mother. And their nanny would be banished forever. It seemed like there was nothing they could do. Their father was whistling happily to himself in his bedroom as he put on his best gray suit. And their future stepmother was happily locked in the garage fixing their father's car.

"It's all over," said Samantha.

"There's nothing we can do," said Derrick.

"We're going to have a stepmother," said Michael.

"There is one last thing we can try," said Nanny Piggins.

"What?" asked the children.

"I'm going to kick in that garage door and bite her on the leg," said Nanny Piggins.

"What good will that do?" asked Samantha.

"It will make me feel better," said Nanny Piggins.

So the children followed Nanny Piggins through

the house as she marched toward the garage. Nanny Piggins had an eighth-degree black belt in taekwondo, so it only took one spinning reverse sidekick to reduce the door to splinters. But Nanny Piggins never bit Jane on the leg; she was too busy staring in stunned silence. Because, as she and the children burst into the garage, they discovered exactly what Jane had been doing in there all that time. She had completely transformed Mr. Green's poo-brown Rolls-Royce. There was now a giant number *23* painted on the side, a roll cage built into the chassis, and support beams welded into the hood and trunk.

"Leaping lamingtons!" exclaimed Nanny Piggins. "You don't love Mr. Green at all! You're only marrying him for his Rolls-Royce."

"Of course," laughed Jane maniacally. "A fool like that doesn't deserve this masterpiece of British engineering. I've seen the way he drives it. Always five miles per hour below the speed limit. Slowing down for yellow lights. Braking for pedestrians. It's practically a crime!"

"So you're going to enter it in a motor race?" asked Nanny Piggins.

"Motor racing is for wimps," said Jane dismissively. "I'm entering it in a demolition derby."

Nanny Piggins gasped.

"What's a demolition derby?" asked Michael.

"It's where ten cars drive into an arena and only one car leaves. They ram and smash each other into oblivion," explained Nanny Piggins.

"And with this car I will be unstoppable," declared Jane.

Nanny Piggins glared at Jane through squinted eyes as though seeing her for the first time. "I only know of one woman who would marry a man just for his car."

"Who?" asked Boris.

"Charlotte Piggins, my twin sister!" declared Nanny Piggins, whipping the horn-rimmed spectacles off Jane Doeadear's face.

The children gasped. Boris fainted. They were looking at an exact replica of Nanny Piggins.

"I knew you looked familiar!" said Nanny Piggins. "You didn't really need glasses for your eyesight. They were just a cunning disguise."

"So this is another one of your identical fourteen-tuplet sisters?" asked Derrick.

"I only know of one woman who would
marry a man just for his car."

"It is indeed," confirmed Nanny Piggins. "This isn't the first time Charlotte's done this either. How many men have you married for their cars now?"

"This will be my eleventh," admitted Charlotte. "I always make sure they put 'to love, honor, and give me a copy of their car keys' into the wedding vows."

"You're practically an evil genius," conceded Nanny Piggins.

"Thank you," said Charlotte.

"Father is going to be so upset when he finds out he's marrying a pig," said Samantha.

"He'll never notice," said Charlotte. "Men are so unobservant."

"But there's no reason to marry him at all," said Nanny Piggins.

"There isn't?" asked Charlotte Piggins.

"I can give you a key to the car," said Nanny Piggins. "I have my own." She took a key to the Rolls-Royce out of her pocket and showed it to her identical twin sister.

"You mean I cleaned his oven for nothing?!" exclaimed Charlotte. "You had a key the whole time?"

"You only had to ask," said Nanny Piggins.

"That's fantastic!" exclaimed Charlotte, snatching

up the keys. "Because there's a bachelor in the next town with a Bentley I've had my eye on."

So Nanny Piggins allowed her sister to drive off at top speed without biting her on the leg, on the condition that she promised to never ever try marrying Mr. Green again.

Mr. Green was naturally devastated. Partly because he lost his fiancée/nanny/domestic slave. But mainly because he lost his poo-brown Rolls-Royce, which was not insured, because Mr. Green was too cheap to pay for insurance.

Nanny Piggins eventually took pity on him because she got tired of listening to him sobbing in his room. She found another Rolls-Royce going for a bargain price (the same color-blind employee who accidentally painted Mr. Green's first Rolls-Royce poo-brown also painted another Rolls-Royce vomit-yellow). So Mr. Green was happy again. As happy as a miser who had just been forced to buy a new car could be. But more importantly, the children were happy because they got to keep their beloved nanny and stay motherless, at least for the time being.

CHAPTER SIX

Nanny Piggins — Holistic Cake Healer

anny Piggins and Michael sat in the doctor's waiting room. Michael was not sick. He simply had a bucket stuck on his head. It was a red plastic bucket, the type you take to the beach and use to build sand castles. It came to be stuck on Michael's head partly because it was so red and tempting, and partly because Nanny Piggins had bet him he could not fit it on there. And being an enthusiastic boy who liked a challenge, Michael won the bet. Which is how he came to be in need of medical attention.

"Can you breathe all right, Michael?" asked Nanny Piggins.

"Yes, so long as I don't eat anything because I can only breathe through my mouth," said Michael. Both his nostrils were entirely sealed because his nose was pressed hard against the inside of the plastic bucket.

"What about angel food cake? It's very light and airy," suggested Nanny Piggins.

"That would probably be all right," conceded Michael.

Nanny Piggins rummaged around in her handbag before finding a slice. "Just take a deep breath before you put it in your mouth, then chew quickly," she advised.

Michael did as he was told, and on the whole he decided angel food cake was worth the risk. He would take oxygen starvation over actual starvation any day.

Nanny Piggins looked around the waiting room. She did not like being made to wait. To have an actual room purely for waiting struck her as a very bad sign. She never had to wait at the ice-cream shop or the bakery. And in her opinion, ice-cream makers and bakers were far more important, busy professionals than doctors.

When they had first arrived at the office, the receptionist had assured Nanny Piggins that they would not have to wait long. But the receptionist's idea of what *long* meant seemed to bear no reference to any commonly understood concept of time. Nanny Piggins wondered if the receptionist's brain was existing in a parallel universe where an hour was really five seconds. Because they had already been waiting for twenty minutes, and in that time no one had come in or gone out of the doctor's room. And as there were six people waiting ahead of Nanny Piggins and Michael, it was clearly going to take forever.

Michael could tell from the tapping of her trotter that his nanny was getting impatient. "Why don't you read a magazine?" he suggested.

Nanny Piggins looked at the dog-eared pile of magazines slumped on the coffee table.

"They are all at least five years old," said Nanny Piggins dismissively.

"So?" questioned Michael.

"The crosswords have been done, all the good recipes have been torn out, and the celebrities in the celebrity gossip articles aren't famous anymore," explained Nanny Piggins.

"Oh," said Michael.

"Plus they've been sitting in a doctor's waiting room for five years, which means every page has five years' worth of germs wiped on them from sick people's hands," declared Nanny Piggins.

"Gross," said Michael.

The patients currently reading magazines began to look uncomfortable.

"I know," said Nanny Piggins. "And just think, some people lick their fingers before they turn the pages."

The other patients now put their magazines down.

"I think I'm going to be sick," said Michael. Under the bucket he was turning a nasty shade of green.

Nanny Piggins looked around the waiting room at the other sick people. Her curiosity was starting to bubble. She turned to a haggard-looking woman sitting next to her. "What's wrong with you?"

"I've got chronic fatigue syndrome," said the haggard-looking woman.

"You've got chronic whatsiewhat?" asked Nanny Piggins.

"I'm tired all the time," explained the woman.

"You know what you need—a big slice of chocolate mud cake every hour on the hour," advised Nanny Piggins.

"But some mornings I can't even get out of bed," said the haggard woman.

"Then get someone to bring the cake to your bed," urged Nanny Piggins. "Better still, put a whole family-sized chocolate mud cake on the pillow next to you before you go to sleep at night. It will be impossible to be tired and depressed when you wake up to that glorious sight in the morning."

"Really?" asked the woman.

"I guarantee it will perk you up," said Nanny Piggins. "Once, when my circus was traveling through India, our lion tamer dropped dead. You have to understand, he was an elderly man and it was a very hot day. But I wafted a slice of chocolate mud cake under his nose and he perked right up again. He tamed lions for another eight years."

"Before he died of old age?" asked the haggard woman.

"No, he was eaten by a lion," said Nanny Piggins, "but that's the way all lion tamers want to go — while putting on a show."

"Thank you," said the haggard woman. "I'm going to try it. The doctor hasn't been much help. And it's so exhausting sitting here waiting. I'm off to the bakery." The haggard woman stood up to leave.

"Here," said Nanny Piggins, offering her a bar of chocolate. "Have some chocolate. It will give you the energy to get to the bakery."

The other patients watched enviously as the woman left.

Nanny Piggins was starting to enjoy herself. It was fun helping people. And now there was one less person ahead of them waiting to see the doctor. Nanny Piggins turned to the elderly man sitting on the other side of Michael.

"What's wrong with you?" asked Nanny Piggins.

"I've got a cold." The elderly man sniffed.

"There's no cure for the common cold," chided Nanny Piggins. "Surely you're old enough to know that."

"But I feel so awful," said the old man. "I thought there might be some way the doctor could help me."

Nanny Piggins rolled her eyes. "For a start, the doctor is not going to help you. They are trained not to do that at medical school. They either cure you and expect you to be grateful, or they don't cure you and expect you to be ashamed for wasting their time," said Nanny Piggins.

"What am I going to do?" asked the old man.

"If you have a cold, the best thing to do is boost your body's natural defenses with vitamin C," instructed Nanny Piggins.

"So I should get some vitamin C tablets?" asked the old man.

"No, I recommend lemon cake at least five times a day," advised Nanny Piggins.

"Lemon cake?" asked the old man.

"Oh yes, it's full of vitamin C. As well as other health foods, like butter and sugar, which are sure to give you a boost," said Nanny Piggins.

"It's worth a try," said the old man. "It's better than waiting endlessly only to be told off for wasting the doctor's time."

So the old man got up and left. Now there were only four people ahead of Michael. Nanny Piggins was getting rid of the other patients effectively. And still no one had come out or gone into the doctor's room yet.

"What do you think he's doing in there?" a pale young woman asked Nanny Piggins. "Why is it taking so long? Do you think he's got someone seriously ill in there?"

"Oh goodness no," said Nanny Piggins. "He's probably got a secret back door out of his office, and he's snuck off to play video games for half an hour."

"Do you think so?" asked the young woman.

"Yes," said Nanny Piggins. "That's what most doctors do. If they could think of some way of charging us all for seeing them without actually seeing them, I'm sure they would."

"I'd go home right now, but my leg hurts so much, I don't know that I could make it that far," said the pale young woman.

"What have you done to yourself?" asked Nanny Piggins.

"I locked myself out of my fifth-floor apartment. And I sprained my ankle trying to climb in through the window," said the young woman.

"You fell five stories?!" exclaimed Nanny Piggins. As a former professional flying pig she had suffered many long falls herself, but even Nanny Piggins was impressed by a five-story fall with nothing more serious than a sprained ankle.

"No, I got up the five stories all right. But when I got in through the window, I fell and landed awkwardly on the dryer," explained the young woman.

"Hard luck," said Nanny Piggins. "Landings are always the hardest part."

"Now my ankle is all swollen," said the young woman, raising her trouser leg to show an unnaturally large, bright red ankle.

"You know what you need?" began Nanny Piggins.

"Some type of cake?" guessed Michael.

"Exactly," said Nanny Piggins. "An ice-cream cake. You can use it as a cold compress on your ankle. But make sure you have a spoon in your hand to eat the ice cream as it melts."

"That's a brilliant idea!" said the young woman as she got up and hobbled to the door.

"Keep your foot elevated and in the fridge!" called

Nanny Piggins. "So the ice cream doesn't melt too quickly." By now the other patients had all perked up and were eagerly awaiting treatment by Nanny Piggins.

And so, in the time it took for the doctor to finish pretending to see one imaginary patient, Nanny Piggins managed to cure a whole waiting room's worth of invalids. Of course, she had a huge advantage over the doctor. Whereas he had gone to medical school and had to learn the names and effects of thousands of drugs, she simply prescribed cake.

When the doctor eventually came out to see his next patient, not even Michael and Nanny Piggins were there. (Between diagnoses, Nanny Piggins had been amusing some small children by reenacting the time she was chased by an ostrich across the African Sahara. She accidentally fell off the coffee table and knocked Michael hard on the back, which made the bucket fly off his head.) The doctor was horrified to discover a completely empty waiting room.

"Why is nobody waiting in my waiting room?" demanded the doctor.

"A pig cured them," explained the receptionist.

"A pig!" exclaimed the doctor. He would have fired

his receptionist on the spot, but he could not because she was his wife. So he had to satisfy himself with stalking back into his office and slamming the door. But then he had to come out again, because the more he thought about it, the more he wanted to know—what pig?

$$\star \quad \star \quad \star$$

Back at the Green house, Nanny Piggins and the children were enjoying a game of tag. Nanny Piggins had discovered that this already excellent game could be dramatically improved by playing it indoors. It added to the excitement to be rushing past Mr. Green's valuable antique furniture and fragile porcelain. So, as you can imagine, they were all having a marvelous time and naturally felt resentful when they heard the front doorbell ring.

"Doorbell," called Michael.

"I suppose we have to answer it," moaned Nanny Piggins.

"It might be someone fun who wants to play tag," said Samantha. She had become a little overexcited about the game and was not thinking clearly.

"In my experience, whenever you're enjoying good loud fun, no one ever knocks on the door to encourage you to have even more fun," said Nanny Piggins sadly.

"I'll answer it," volunteered Derrick. "If it's someone who's come to complain about the noise, I'll just say we're burglars and we don't live here."

"Good idea," approved Nanny Piggins.

As it turned out they were partly right. When Derrick opened the door, the man on the step had come to complain, but not about the noise. It was the doctor.

"Is there a pig living here?" asked the doctor rudely. For even though he had not said anything technically rude, he had the knack of making otherwise polite sentences sound rude.

"Maybe," said Derrick, not wanting to get his nanny in trouble.

"I want to speak to her," demanded the doctor.

"That's nice," said Derrick, shutting the door in his face.

The doctor knocked on the door again. Derrick opened it again.

"I said I wanted to speak to the pig," snapped the doctor.

"Well, we don't always get what we want, do we?" said Derrick, swinging the door shut again.

The doctor knocked on the door yet again. Derrick opened it yet again. The doctor took a deep breath and through gritted teeth said, "Please may I speak to Miss Piggins?" After all, he was not a stupid man, just a slow learner.

"Wait here," said Derrick, shutting the door on the doctor for a third time.

The doctor waited on the doorstep for forty-five minutes before the door swung open again. He was really furious. The doctor drew in his breath to start yelling, but then he stopped because right in front of him stood the most beautiful pig he had ever seen. He had to pause and think for a moment. When he had imagined himself yelling at a pig, the pig he had imagined had not looked like this at all. The pig of his imagination certainly had not been wearing designer clothes and eye makeup. Derrick, Samantha, and Michael stood behind Nanny Piggins, waiting to see what she would do to the doctor.

"Did you enjoy that?" asked Nanny Piggins.

"Did I enjoy what?" asked the doctor, having no idea what she was talking about.

"Waiting," said Nanny Piggins.

"No, it's very rude to leave me standing out here for so long," complained the doctor.

"Exactly," said Nanny Piggins. "Now you know what it's like. I hope you don't make your patients wait so long in the future."

"But that's different," spluttered the doctor. "They have a comfortable waiting room with magazines."

"Don't get her started on the magazines," advised Michael. "It will make you feel sick."

"There is nothing comfortable about putting a group of diseased people in a confined space and leaving them there for an hour," argued Nanny Piggins.

"Look here, you have completely ruined my business," complained the doctor.

"Have I?" asked Nanny Piggins.

"All my patients have left me and taken up eating cake," said the doctor.

"I'm sure they're a lot happier," said Nanny Piggins.

"That's not the point," protested the doctor. "It is my job to make sure they are well."

"You're not doing a very good job, then," said Nanny Piggins.

"I spent six years at medical school learning to be a doctor," said the doctor. "You can't come along and steal all my patients by prescribing cake!"

"Oh, can't I?" said Nanny Piggins, her eyes narrowing.

This just goes to show how very unwise the doctor was. Because anyone who knew Nanny Piggins knew that you should never ever tell her she could not do something. Once, one of the acrobats at the circus had made a similar mistake. He'd said Nanny Piggins would never be able to pogo-jump all the way across Belgium dressed up as Henry the Eighth. Three days, two million jumps, and one very sweaty Henry the Eighth costume later, he was made to look very silly indeed. Telling Nanny Piggins she could not do something was always the best way to make sure that was exactly what she did.

Indeed, humans underestimating the willpower of pigs is a common theme throughout history. It was a pig who built the Great Wall of China to keep the Mongol hordes from invading. (Which is why to this day in every Chinese restaurant you get Mongolian beef, not Mongolian pork.) And it was a pig who discovered America, but, unlike Christopher Columbus, she had the good sense to keep her discovery to herself because she found lots of yummy food there.

Nanny Piggins had planned to spend the next day setting up a ham radio and gossiping with her friends on the Falkland Islands. But the doctor had annoyed her, so she decided to annoy him back.

The next morning, when the doctor arrived at his office, there were, yet again, no patients waiting.

"Where are all my patients today?" ranted the doctor. His wife/receptionist did not bother explaining; she just pointed out the window. There, on the other side of the road, sat Nanny Piggins. She had set up a cake stall with a sign overhead reading HOLISTIC CAKE HEALER. And, unlike the doctor, she was surrounded by eager patients, keen to try her New Age style of healing.

"Now she's gone too far!" exploded the doctor.

He set out across the street to give Nanny Piggins a piece of his mind. "You cannot treat ill people purely by giving them cake!" he yelled at Nanny Piggins.

"I know," said Nanny Piggins. "That's why I'm branching out."

"You're what?" spluttered the doctor.

"You cannot treat ill people purely
by giving them cake!" he yelled at
Nanny Piggins.

"I'm using honey to treat wounds," started Nanny Piggins.

"It's an excellent antiseptic," supplied Samantha.

"Lemonade to treat sore throats," said Nanny Piggins.

"It's very soothing," added Boris.

"And I'm using fudge to treat irritable bowel syndrome," said Nanny Piggins.

The doctor was momentarily flummoxed. He did not know what to take exception to first: being spoken to by a ten-foot-tall bear or hearing bizarre medical advice from a pig. In the end his curiosity got the better of him. "How does fudge help irritable bowel syndrome?"

"It doesn't," explained Nanny Piggins, "but it really cheers the patient up."

"Why are you trying to ruin my business?" asked the doctor.

"I'm not," said Nanny Piggins. "I'm merely trying to supply a better alternative."

"Cake, lemonade, and fudge are no alternative to clinical medicine," complained the doctor.

"Maybe not, but it is a quicker alternative," said Nanny Piggins. "And people are tired of waiting in your waiting room."

"This won't last," prophesied the doctor. "My patients will come back. They will have their cake, but they will want their medicine too."

With that, the doctor stormed back to his office and sat inside, sulking, as Nanny Piggins did a roaring trade, selling cake and sweet goods all day long.

★ ★ ★

As I am sure you have already guessed, the doctor was completely wrong. Three days later, his waiting room was still completely empty and Nanny Piggins's cake stall was still thriving. He sat in his office, looking out the window and feeling very sorry for himself. For the first time in twenty years of practicing medicine, a thought occurred to him that had never occurred to him before: Maybe he was not as important as he thought he was. It was a very depressing idea. It made him feel all hollow and empty inside. His eyes started to itch. A lump formed in his throat. Then the doctor realized what he needed. He needed a piece of cake to cheer himself up.

And so the doctor swallowed his pride because he

wanted to swallow some cake. He crossed the street and approached Nanny Piggins, looking very sad.

"What do you want?" asked Nanny Piggins.

"A slice of lemon drizzle cake please," mumbled the doctor.

Nanny Piggins considered torturing him some more, pretending she had run out of cake and making him beg for it. But she could see he was a broken man. So, being a compassionate pig, she cut him a large slice (and a slice that Nanny Piggins considered large was very large indeed).

"A lesser pig would tell you to go away. But when I became a holistic cake healer, I took the Hippopigic Oath—swearing to never withhold cake from anyone who needed it, no matter who they were, how rude they were, or how long they kept their patients waiting in their waiting room."

"That seems an awfully specific oath," said the doctor.

"Do you want your cake or not?" snapped Nanny Piggins.

And the doctor hurriedly took it. As soon as he swallowed his first bite, he started to feel better. "So are you going to have your cake stall here forever, then?" he asked resignedly.

"Perhaps not quite forever," admitted Nanny Piggins.

"You're not?" asked the doctor, now starting to really brighten up.

"Much as I enjoy being a holistic cake healer, it isn't really my calling," said Nanny Piggins.

"It's not?" asked the doctor, actually starting to smile again, in between shoveling mouthfuls of lemon drizzle cake into his mouth.

"You see, I have a career dilemma. While I am very good at prescribing cake, my true talent lies elsewhere. I have an even greater gift for eating cake," said Nanny Piggins immodestly but truthfully. "It presents a terrible conflict of interest."

"It does?" said the doctor. Now he almost wanted to kiss Nanny Piggins he was so grateful.

"Tell him the real reason you want to give up being a holistic cake healer, Nanny Piggins," chided Samantha.

Nanny Piggins looked away shiftily. "I don't know what you're talking about."

"You're going to need the doctor's help to solve the problem," prompted Derrick.

143

"You have a problem I can help with?" said the doctor, now positively gleeful.

"No," said Nanny Piggins petulantly.

"Lying is wrong," Michael reminded her.

"All right, all right! I'll admit it. My patients have been coming down with a few problems," confessed Nanny Piggins.

"Oh dear," said the doctor.

"They are very happy with my treatment. And I always cure their problem. But holistic cake therapy seems to have an unfortunate side effect," said Nanny Piggins.

"What side effect?" asked the doctor.

"Stomachache," said Derrick matter-of-factly.

"Ah," said the doctor knowingly, struggling hard not to look smug.

"I tried prescribing more cake," said Nanny Piggins. "That always works for me when I have a stomachache."

"I see," said the doctor.

"I tell the patients—all you have to do is tough it out and push through the cake barrier. If you just keep eating cake, eventually your body becomes so high on sugar and numb from overeating that you start to feel all right again. But for some reason, it doesn't seem to work for all my patients."

"Perhaps," suggested the doctor diplomatically, "because they are not pigs?"

"I suppose that might have something to do with it," conceded Nanny Piggins. "Humans can be very weak sometimes."

"It's our own fault," said the doctor humbly. "We're not lucky enough to have your superior digestive capabilities."

"True," acknowledged Nanny Piggins.

And so Nanny Piggins and the doctor came to an agreement. She would stop being a holistic cake healer right outside his office. And he would make sure he saw all his patients as promptly as possible. No more sneaking out the back door to play video games. (He admitted that was what he had been doing.) And if for some unforeseen reason, a patient did have to wait for more than ten minutes, the doctor would provide them with a slice of cake—one for every ten minutes they were delayed, until he was able to see them.

This regimen worked beautifully. All the doctor's patients returned. They were glad to be seen more promptly. And they were even more glad when he could not see them promptly because they enjoyed eating cake. Indeed, sometimes, when they were hungry, Nanny Piggins and the children went along and sat in the waiting room even when there was nothing wrong with them, just so they could have a slice of cake too.

CHAPTER SEVEN

Nanny Piggins and the Fat Lady

anny Piggins was relaxing in the bath. She had been in there so long, her skin was even pinker than usual and the paperback she was reading had fallen in the water three times. So, as she read, she had to carefully peel back each page or she might tear it (and subsequently never find out who murdered Mrs. Bottomly in the conservatory with a pair of long-handled garden shears). Nanny Piggins had one rule when she was in the bath: "Don't interrupt me unless you're bringing a snack."

So when a noise disturbed her and Nanny Piggins looked up to see a chocolate bar sliding under the door, she knew one of the children was outside and wanted to speak to her.

"Yes?" said Nanny Piggins. (She was curt because she was not entirely ready to tear herself away from the world of crime and mystery just yet.)

"Nanny Piggins, there was someone at the door," said Derrick.

"Well, if they've gone away, what's the problem?" asked Nanny Piggins, still furtively reading to find out if her suspicions were true, and that Cousin Gertrude, the physicist, was the one who'd put the poison in the gardener's hot chocolate.

"He was at the door; now he's climbing up the drainpipe," explained Derrick.

"The Ringmaster!" exclaimed Nanny Piggins as she leaped out of the bath. For she knew only one man impertinent enough to take a closed front door as an invitation to climb up the outside of the building and in through an upstairs window.

And indeed, she had barely wrapped herself in her robe before the bathroom window was shoved open and the Ringmaster's fat bottom started to wiggle its way into the room. Nanny Piggins instinctively picked up the toilet brush and hit him hard. (Nanny Piggins would never dream of spanking children. But in her professional opinion most fully grown men could do with a good spanking at least once a day.)

Surprisingly, the Ringmaster did not say "Ow!" although we must presume he thought it. Instead he turned to Nanny Piggins with the most sickeningly insincere smile on his face and said, "Sarah Piggins, what a wonderful surprise!" Then he kissed her loudly on each cheek. To which Nanny Piggins naturally responded by stomping hard on his foot. (This was the way Nanny Piggins and the Ringmaster always greeted each other. There was a time when Nanny Piggins would go to the trouble of biting his leg every time they met. But one day she got a piece of his trousers caught between her teeth and she had to go to the dentist, so she did not risk that anymore.)

"I am not coming back to your circus to be a flying pig again," declared Nanny Piggins boldly.

"I wouldn't dream of it," lied the Ringmaster.

"Really? Well, I know for a fact that my sister

Katerina, who replaced me as your flying pig, has recently run away from you," said Nanny Piggins.

"That was entirely my own fault," said the Ringmaster. "Given her inexplicable love of vegetables, I should never have taken the circus to Wales. The local leeks were always going to be impossible for her to resist."

"True," agreed Nanny Piggins. Katerina was obsessed when it came to green vegetables. "But I'm still not going back to being a flying pig." (Not that Nanny Piggins minded the actual flying part of being a flying pig. She just did not enjoy the no-hot-and-cold-running-water part of living in a circus.)

"There is no need for you to return to the circus," said the Ringmaster. "We have replaced your sister with a flying chicken."

"What's so remarkable about a flying chicken?" asked Nanny Piggins. "All chickens can fly."

"We put the chicken in a pig costume," explained the Ringmaster.

"Ah," said Nanny Piggins. This made perfect sense. "So why exactly have you invaded my private bathroom? Give me one good reason why I shouldn't hit you with the toilet brush again."

"I've just come to catch up with a dear old friend," said the Ringmaster.

"Who?" asked Nanny Piggins.

"You," said the Ringmaster.

Nanny Piggins hit the Ringmaster on the leg with the toilet brush just for good measure. "You know perfectly well we are not good friends, but archenemies."

"Are you all right in there, Nanny Piggins?" asked Samantha from the other side of the bathroom door. "Would you like us to call the police or something?"

"I'd like you to fetch me the fire poker," said Nanny Piggins. "The toilet brush doesn't seem to hurt enough."

"All right, I'll admit I was wondering if you could do me a little favor. Not so much for me, but for another dear friend of mine who is having a terrible career crisis," said the Ringmaster.

"If she works for you, I'm not surprised she's having a career crisis," said Nanny Piggins, who had herself chewed through a thick canvas tent and stolen an Indian elephant in her bid to escape the Ringmaster's workplace.

"She's waiting outside. I'll bring her in," said the Ringmaster. "Would you like to dress and come downstairs, or should I get her to climb up and in through the bathroom window?"

Nanny Piggins whacked the Ringmaster one more time for his impertinence, then followed him downstairs. She did not get dressed, because she knew if she took her eyes off the Ringmaster for two seconds, the children would go missing and turn up three months later in Belarus working as trapeze artists. It was not so much that the Ringmaster was evil (although he certainly was) as that he could not help himself. Being a true showman, he was always recruiting new talent whether they wanted to be recruited or not.

Nanny Piggins and the children sat in the living room, waiting for the Ringmaster to return with his troubled protégé. Boris was there too, but he was still frightened of the Ringmaster, so he hid underneath the hearth rug.

The Ringmaster returned a few moments later with a woman. But to call her a woman is not really fair for women in general. Because she was so dazzlingly beautiful and gorgeous it was as if she belonged to another species. She had all the stereotypical attributes associated with beauty. She was tall and skinny, and

Boris was there too, but he was still frightened of the Ringmaster, so he hid underneath the hearth rug.

her hair was so shiny it looked like it had been painted with decking oil. Nanny Piggins's instinct was to hate her immediately. But then the tall, thin, beautiful woman shocked Nanny Piggins by saying "Sarah Piggins, how wonderful to see you again!" and giving her a big hug.

Nanny Piggins wished she had brought the toilet brush downstairs so she could hit this strange woman too. "I've never seen you before in my life," declared Nanny Piggins.

"Oh yes, you have," said the Ringmaster. "It's Lavinia."

"You remember me, don't you? From the circus?" asked Lavinia.

Nanny Piggins squinted at Lavinia closely. "The only Lavinia I know was Lavinia the Fat Lady."

"Exactly. That's the problem. This is my Fat Lady," said the Ringmaster, pointing at Lavinia with disgust.

Lavinia looked ashamed of herself.

"No!" gasped Nanny Piggins. "The last time I saw you, you weighed eight hundred pounds."

"Hey," came the muffled cry of Boris from under the carpet.

"Not that that's a lot," said Nanny Piggins hastily, for she did not want to hurt her brother's feelings. Boris weighed over a thousand pounds and was very sensitive about the subject.

Nanny Piggins looked Lavinia up and down. "What happened to you? Did you get some sort of intestinal parasite? Or did an evil villain lock you in a cellar and force you to eat oatmeal?" Nanny Piggins eyed the Ringmaster as she said this. It was just the type of thing he would do.

"No," said Lavinia. She was obviously both embarrassed and ashamed.

"Tell her," said the Ringmaster sternly.

"Do I have to?" pleaded Lavinia.

"If she is going to help you, she needs to know the truth," said the Ringmaster.

"But I'm so ashamed," protested Lavinia.

"All the more reason to come clean," said the Ringmaster.

"My aunt—" Lavinia broke off as she started to sob.

"Spit it out," urged the Ringmaster.

"My aunt gave me an aerobics video for Christmas," admitted Lavinia, breaking into tears.

Nanny Piggins gasped.

Boris gasped. Then he choked and coughed because he had sucked in a mouthful of dust under the carpet.

"What was she thinking?" asked Nanny Piggins. "You're a Fat Lady!"

"I know," said Lavinia the Fat Lady.

"Tell her the rest," said the Ringmaster severely.

"There's more?" asked Nanny Piggins, who did not think she could be more shocked.

"I went on a diet," admitted Lavinia.

"No!" exclaimed Nanny Piggins.

"*Nyet!*" exclaimed Boris, who was so shocked he reverted to speaking in Russian.

"And..." cajoled the Ringmaster. "Tell her everything."

"I started jogging," admitted Lavinia as tears of shame rolled down her cheeks.

"You poor, poor woman," said Nanny Piggins, taking Lavinia in her arms and giving her a hug.

"I don't know what to do," sobbed Lavinia. "I've ruined my career. Being a Fat Lady is all I know."

"Don't worry," said Nanny Piggins comfortingly. "You've come to the right place. We will help you.

You'll soon be so disgustingly fat, people will pay to point at you and stare again."

"Do you think so?" asked Lavinia hopefully.

"No one knows more about eating high-calorie food than Nanny Piggins," Michael assured her.

"Thank you, thank you so much," wept Lavinia.

"Excellent!" exclaimed the Ringmaster. "Lavinia needs to be five times her current body weight by a week from Friday because we're taking the circus to Morocco."

"Get out of this house before I risk my teeth and bite you on the leg," said Nanny Piggins.

Fortunately Nanny Piggins did not have to carry out her threat because the Ringmaster had already done a commando leap out of the living room window and was running off down the street.

Nanny Piggins turned and looked at the sorry sight of the svelte and beautiful Fat Lady. "I hardly know where to begin," said Nanny Piggins. "Yes, I do! Lie down," ordered Nanny Piggins.

"What, here on the floor?" asked Lavinia the thin Fat Lady.

"Just do it! Right now. You have to stop exercising

immediately. Standing up is burning too many calories," declared Nanny Piggins.

Lavinia dropped to the floor. Because, despite being thin and beautiful on the outside, she was fat at heart, and as such, very kind and obedient.

"But how am I going to get around?" asked Lavinia from her position on the floor.

"Boris will carry you," said Nanny Piggins.

"Boris?!" said Lavinia and Boris simultaneously. Lavinia because she had not realized that Boris was there, and Boris because he did not realize that Lavinia not doing exercise meant he was going to have to start doing exercise.

"Look at her, Boris. She's so thin. She desperately needs your help," said Nanny Piggins.

Boris poked his head out from under the carpet and got his first look at Lavinia. He had to admit she was skinny. "I'll barely notice carrying her," said Boris.

"He carried a hitchhiker around for a week without noticing," explained Michael.

"I actually ended up noticing the smell. He didn't bathe as often as he should have," added Boris.

Lavinia was delighted to see Boris. They were old

friends from the circus and would often share a gallon of honey together. "I didn't realize you were hiding under the carpet, Boris. I thought Nanny Piggins had just swept a lot of rubbish under there."

"Oh no. I would never do that. I always sweep the rubbish under the carpet behind the couch. It's much less noticeable," said Nanny Piggins, pointing to an even lumpier carpet on the other side of the room.

"Where do we start?" asked Lavinia.

"The first thing we need to do is go to the bakery and buy some cakes," decided Nanny Piggins.

"Because eating cake is a good way to gain weight?" asked Samantha.

"No, because eating cake helps you think," said Nanny Piggins. "But I suppose it will be good for that too."

And so Nanny Piggins, Boris, Lavinia, and the children walked down to the bakery. Boris pushed Lavinia in a wheelbarrow so she would not burn any calories, but she could look around and point at things she might like to eat.

They stood outside the bakery, looking in through the window at the display of cakes for some time. Nanny Piggins believed buying cake was a serious decision-making process that should never be rushed. Fortunately Hans the baker was very understanding about it. He employed a full-time staff member, Emily, just for cleaning the marks customers left from pressing their noses against his window. (All truly good bakeries have to.)

"If Lavinia is going to gain hundreds and hundreds of pounds, she is going to have to eat a lot of cake," said Samantha.

"Of course," said Nanny Piggins. "We will all have to eat a lot of cake. Because it would be unsupportive to force Lavinia to do it all on her own."

"But how are we going to afford all that cake?" asked Samantha.

"Fortunately, I had the foresight to sell one of your father's valuable tax law books on the Internet last night," said Nanny Piggins. "I put the dust jacket around one of my romance novels so he'll never realize it's gone."

"You did?" asked Derrick, feeling both horrified and thrilled at the same time.

"Yes, I sell something of his every time he irritates me. So I usually sell five or six things of his every night. On Tuesday last week, when he complained that I hadn't ironed his underwear, I sold seventeen pairs of his cuff links," said Nanny Piggins.

"But what if Father finds out?" asked Michael.

"He won't, not if I sell all his shirts with French cuffs next," said Nanny Piggins. "Come on, let's go inside and place our order."

They all went into the shop.

"What would you like, Lavinia?" asked Nanny Piggins.

"A salad," said Lavinia, without realizing what she was saying. Her hands flew to her mouth as if to catch the already-escaped words. "I'm so sorry. I don't know what came over me." Tears welled in her eyes.

"It's all right, dear," said Nanny Piggins firmly. "We're here to help you. Let me make the decisions." Nanny Piggins proceeded to order enough cake, meringue, and doughnuts to give a battalion of soldiers a sugar high for twelve months. Hans the baker soon realized he would have to hire a full-size moving truck to bring all the cake to the Green house. But Nanny Piggins was far and away his best customer, so it would be worth the extra cost.

Back at the Green house Nanny Piggins was ready to commence phase two—the eating. Nanny Piggins drew up a schedule so she, Boris, and the children could take turns feeding Lavinia. Lavinia had offered to feed herself, but Nanny Piggins would not let her. She was concerned that picking up the food and putting it in her mouth would burn too many calories. Chewing was obviously a problem. Nanny Piggins had tried to think of a way to get around Lavinia having to chew. All that up and down movement of her jaw was bound to use energy. But all the solutions to bypass chewing were too disgusting to consider.

Things progressed well for the first seven hours. Lavinia might be thin and beautiful, but she had been a professional Fat Lady for many years and she still had impressive eating skills. Once a woman learns to shove an entire cream-covered pavlova[5] in her mouth, that is a talent she never loses. So the eating went smoothly

---

[5] A pavlova is a large meringue-based dessert invented in New Zealand and named after the great ballerina Anna Pavlova. It does not contain a single ingredient that is good for you. Unless someone adds fruit to the top for decorative reasons, but you can always pick that off.

until night fell and it was Michael's turn to do the hand-feeding.

Now you must remember that Michael was only seven. Which was not his fault. He had no say in when he was born. And the thing about seven-year-olds, indeed all young children, is that when they fall asleep, they really fall asleep. People in comas sleep less soundly than the average seven-year-old. Nanny Piggins believed this was because of all the boring things that seven-year-olds are forced to learn at school. They have to sleep soundly while their brains try to expel the useless information.

At any rate, when Nanny Piggins came downstairs to commence her five AM feeding shift, she found Michael fast asleep at the kitchen table and Lavinia nowhere to be seen. Nanny Piggins was just about to panic when Lavinia slipped in the back door. "Good morning, Nanny Piggins. I just stepped outside to see if the sun was up yet," said Lavinia the thin Fat Lady.

"Really?" asked Nanny Piggins, squinting at her. "And what have I told you about walking?"

"I'm sorry," apologized Lavinia guiltily.

Nanny Piggins suspected Lavinia had been up to something. "You do know that pigs have an incredibly acute sense of smell?"

"No, I didn't realize that," admitted Lavinia nervously.

"We can smell aromas so faint even a large-nosed dog can't imagine them," continued Nanny Piggins.

"Really?" said Lavinia. Now she was beginning to look nervous.

"Like, for example," said Nanny Piggins, "I can smell the sweat of a very naughty woman who has secretly been out jogging when she was supposed to be at home getting fat!"

"All right, I admit it. I've been out jogging!" confessed Lavinia.

Nanny Piggins sniffed at Lavinia. "And—"

"And I did some jumping jacks," Lavinia admitted.

"One hundred and fifty-three, if my nose tells me correctly," said Nanny Piggins.

"Actually one hundred and fifty-four," said Lavinia.

"Well, it is first thing in the morning. My snout is just warming up," said Nanny Piggins.

Lavinia broke down in tears. "I'm sorry, Nanny

Piggins. I thought I had the strength to do it, but not being on a diet is so hard."

"There, there," said Nanny Piggins. "You don't have to eat four thousand chocolate cakes if you don't want to."

"I don't?" said Lavinia, starting to look happy for the first time since she had arrived.

"Of course not," said Nanny Piggins. "I'm not the Ringmaster. I don't believe in forcing people into a life of glamour and show business if that's not what they want."

"I liked being a Fat Lady," said Lavinia. "But for some reason I like being thin, fit, and beautiful even more."

"I can't understand it myself," said Nanny Piggins, shaking her head. "But if that's what you want, then that's what you should do."

"But what about the Ringmaster?" asked Lavinia. "I've signed a fifty-year binding contract promising to be over eight hundred pounds for life."

"Him and his diabolical contracts. We'll find a way around it," said Nanny Piggins.

"But how?" asked Lavinia.

"We'll just have to find a replacement. A woman who does enjoy eating three times her body weight in cake a day," said Nanny Piggins.

"Where would we find such a woman?" asked Lavinia.

"By consulting an expert," said Nanny Piggins.

"Who?" asked Lavinia.

"Hans the baker, of course," said Nanny Piggins.

And so Nanny Piggins, Boris, the children, and Lavinia went back to the bakery. And Nanny Piggins let Lavinia walk this time. Boris carried Derrick, Samantha, and Michael instead because he found he liked being a form of transport.

Nanny Piggins asked Hans if he knew of a woman with a great love of cake.

"You mean other than yourself?" asked Hans.

"I already have a job," said Nanny Piggins. "Besides, for some reason, people don't find fat pigs as remarkable as fat women."

"We live in a cruel and prejudiced society," agreed Boris.

"Boris weighs over a thousand pounds and nobody notices because he has such good bone structure," said

Michael. Boris blushed with pleasure at such a lovely compliment.

"So do you know anyone suitable?" asked Nanny Piggins.

"No, I'm sorry," said Hans. "Obviously I know a lot of women who like cake and a lot who even love cake, but I don't think I know a woman who loves cake so much she wants to be a Fat Lady."

Suddenly there was a desperate banging at the window. They all turned around to see Emily (the girl whose job it was to clean nose marks off the glass), desperately beating on the window and pleading, "What about me?!!"

"I think she's trying to tell us something," said Nanny Piggins.

They rushed outside to talk to her. (Emily was not allowed to come inside, because she had to remain vigilant. There were so many people who could, at any moment, press their noses to Hans's window.)

"Do you know someone who would like to be a Fat Lady?" Nanny Piggins asked Emily.

"Yes, me! Being a Fat Lady would be my dream job!" exclaimed Emily.

"Are you sure?" asked Lavinia. "It isn't all eating cake and eclairs and lying around. Well, come to think of it, it is. But that isn't as easy as it sounds."

"I'm certain it's what I want to do," explained Emily. "For seven years I have worked here, cleaning other people's nose marks off this window. And for seven long years I have looked at these cakes, desperately wanting to eat them myself."

"I would have thought you would grow tired of cake working in a bakery," said Samantha.

Nanny Piggins and Emily gasped in horror.

"Samantha, I love you. But I have never before felt such a strong urge to wash your mouth out with soap," said Nanny Piggins.

"Sorry," said Samantha.

"That's all right. I forgive you," said Nanny Piggins, giving Samantha a hug.

"I never ever get tired of cake. Just look at them," said Emily, turning to look at the window display. There was a beautiful array of cakes, tortes, flans, doughnuts, and meringues. "Sometimes when nobody is looking, I actually lick the glass."

And so Emily and Lavinia happily swapped lives.

Emily was so happy to become a Fat Lady, Nanny Piggins had to bite her hard on the hand to stop her from signing one of the Ringmaster's diabolical fifty-year binding contracts. The Ringmaster was happy because, given Emily's enthusiasm for her new job, he suspected he would soon have a nine-hundred-pound Fat Lady, and that would really draw the crowds. And Lavinia was happy too, because finally she was able to cut back her eating to just seven or eight meals a day.[6]

Later that evening, Nanny Piggins, Boris, and the children sat around the television feeling proud of their good works. Only Samantha had one small concern. "Nanny Piggins, don't you feel the slightest bit guilty about encouraging Emily to get really fat? It's not very healthy."

"True, being fat is not healthy," said Nanny Piggins. "But being unhappy is not healthy either. And almost everybody is unhealthy in some way. Marathon runners wreck their knees. Scuba divers get nitrogen narcosis. Flying pigs can accidentally land on asphalt roads and get some very nasty grazes. You see, life is all about

---

[6] She even went on to write an internationally successful diet book called *How to Lose Weight by Not Eating Twenty-Four Cakes a Day.*

choice. It's true that eating cake is not healthy. But if you are really, really good at eating cake, it is a shame to keep your talent from the world."

Nanny Piggins could be a very wise pig. This made so much sense to the children that they never let it worry them again.[7]

---

[7] Dear Reader, I know it is hard to read this book without itching to eat cake, chocolate, and candy. And it is okay to eat those foods in moderation. But remember, it is important that you look after your own health and eat wisely. I want you to live long, happy, healthy lives, so be aware that Nanny Piggins and Emily are not good role models when it comes to eating. (And in case you're wondering, yes, my publisher is forcing me to write this.)

CHAPTER EIGHT

Nanny Piggins and the Stinking, Odorous Lumps

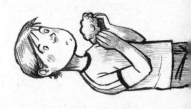

anny Piggins was walking the children to school. The children usually caught the bus. But on this particular morning, Nanny Piggins had been getting to a good bit in her novel, and she had not wanted to get out of bed until she made sure the heroine was not going to be run over by a steam train. (She had been tied to the train tracks by a wicked villain, which was a common problem for heroines before the invention of the motorcar.) By the time Nanny Piggins did get up to whip together a breakfast of homemade jelly doughnuts (with extra jelly and extra doughnut), the school bus was long gone.

Now most people, when they are walking to school, just trudge along in morose silence wishing they were back in bed. But not Nanny Piggins. They had only been walking for a few minutes when suddenly she stopped, grabbed Derrick and Samantha for support, and shrieked, "Ew yuck pooey!!!"

"What is it?" asked Derrick with genuine concern.

"Can't you smell it? It's horrible!" said Nanny Piggins as she tried to hold her trotters over her snout.

"I can't smell anything," said Samantha.

"It's not me," said Michael defensively. "I had a bath yesterday or the day before. I've definitely had one this week!"

"Ew pooey! It's not you. It's something far worse than little-boy smell," said Nanny Piggins.

"Are you sure?" asked Samantha. "Little boys can smell pretty bad."

Derrick and Michael glared at her. "Well, it's true," she maintained.

"No, this is something a thousand times more

horrid," said Nanny Piggins. "Yuck! I wish I had something to stick up my nostrils. Michael, do you still have that banana in your schoolbag?"

"But I want to eat my banana at recess," protested Michael.

"I have a greater need!" insisted Nanny Piggins.

"Come on, Michael, you know if Nanny Piggins had a banana and you wanted to shove it up your nose, she'd give it to you," chided Derrick.

"All right," said Michael, handing over his banana. He was not too reluctant. He had never seen a pig with a banana up her snout before.

"Ahhh, that's better, thank you," said Nanny Piggins, recomposing herself, and assuming all the dignity that a pig with half a banana up each nostril can muster. "Now it only smells utterly disgusting, instead of earth-shatteringly awful."

"Shall we keep walking, then?" suggested Derrick.

"Of course not," said Nanny Piggins. "That would be irresponsible. We can't just let such a sickening stench go unchecked."

"Why not?" asked Michael.

"Who knows where it might waft next?" said

Nanny Piggins darkly. "No, we have to deal with it. Does anybody have a shovel?"

None of the children had a shovel on them.

"Never mind," said Nanny Piggins. "I'll just use my trotters. Now, where is it…?" Nanny Piggins used her banana-stuffed snout to sniff around. The children followed her as she sniffed across the road, under a car, into someone's front yard, around the side of their house, and into the backyard, and stopped right underneath a hazelnut tree.

"Here it is," said Nanny Piggins. "Here's the source of the foul odor."

"I still can't smell anything," said Derrick.

"Can't any of you smell it?" asked Nanny Piggins.

Samantha and Michael shook their heads.

"It's a wonder humans can get anything done when their sense of smell is worse than a blind person's sense of sight," marveled Nanny Piggins as she rolled up her sleeves, got down on the ground, and started digging. The children watched in fascinated awe. Nanny Piggins had a gift for earthworks. Soil flew everywhere as she burrowed downward. Then suddenly, she stopped.

"Aha!" exclaimed Nanny Piggins. "I've got it. And

it's a particularly large one." Nanny Piggins held aloft a large knobbly brown lump about the size of a tennis ball.

"What is it?" asked Michael.

"The worst type of fungus there is," said Nanny Piggins. "A truffle."

"That's a truffle!" exclaimed Derrick.

"Wow!" said Samantha.

"Yes, it's the one drawback of being a pig. I can smell these from miles away," said Nanny Piggins. "Now, do any of you have some matches so we can burn it?"

"You can't burn a truffle!" protested Samantha.

"Why not?" asked Nanny Piggins. "It can't make the smell any worse."

"No, you can't burn truffles because they're incredibly valuable," explained Derrick. He knew this because their father had once tried to avoid paying taxes by hiding a large amount of money in an offshore truffle trading scheme. (Sadly, Mr. Green had lost all this money when a cleaner had mistaken the truffles for rotten mushrooms and fed them to her dogs.)

"This foul-smelling stinky lump is valuable?" asked Nanny Piggins. "To whom?"

"Chefs," explained Derrick. "They use it in cooking."

"They let this near food?!" exclaimed Nanny Piggins. Now she was really shocked.

"They are supposed to be delicious," said Samantha.

"You're pulling my trotter," said Nanny Piggins suspiciously.

"No, it's true," said Samantha. "That lump you've got there is probably worth two or three hundred dollars."

"I don't believe it!" said Nanny Piggins.

That a pungent brown lump of fungus was valuable was too much for Nanny Piggins's brain to accept. So she decided to consult an expert. Nanny Piggins went with the children to see the greatest chef at the finest restaurant in town, Pierre Valjean of the Très Bien French restaurant.

"What do you make of that?" asked Nanny Piggins as she dumped the truffle in front of the famous chef.

"*Sacre boeuf!*" (which is French for "Holy cow!") exclaimed Pierre.

"These children are trying to tell me this smelly thing is valuable. And they don't usually lie, so I am tempted to believe them," said Nanny Piggins.

"Valuable! No, this is priceless!" exclaimed Pierre.

"I knew it!" said Nanny Piggins. "Where's your toilet? I'll flush it away."

"*Non!*" (which is French for "No!") exclaimed Pierre, clutching the truffle to his chest. "When I say priceless, I mean no price is too high."

"That's a funny way of saying it," said Nanny Piggins. "*Worthless* means 'worthless,' so why doesn't *priceless* mean 'priceless'?"

"The English language is very strange," said Michael. He knew this because Boris often said so.

"With this truffle I can make the finest sauces, the most delicate gravies, the most mouthwatering marinades," gushed Pierre.

"So you'd like it, then?" asked Nanny Piggins. "Because I know where we can get more."

"More?" exclaimed Pierre. "I will take all the truffles you have. If I can find a large supply of truffles, I will be able to transform my menu and serve the very finest cuisine."

"The things you humans will eat never ceases to amaze me," said Nanny Piggins, shaking her head.

As Nanny Piggins led the children back out onto the street, she was looking thoughtful.

"So what did you do with all the truffles you found over the years?" asked Derrick.

"Well, some of them I burned," admitted Nanny Piggins.

The children gasped.

"Some of them I flushed down the toilet," said Nanny Piggins.

The children went pale.

"But most of them I buried in a deep hole," said Nanny Piggins.

This made the children feel slightly more cheerful.

"So somewhere there is a big hole full of lots of truffles?" asked Derrick.

"Exactly," said Nanny Piggins. "One weekend I made a point of finding as many of the smelly things as I could and then burying them deep underground."

"Then all we have to do is go and dig them up, and we can sell them for a fortune!" said Derrick.

"The only problem is," said Nanny Piggins, "I'm not entirely sure where the truffle dump is. All those foul-smelling truffles affect my sense of direction. It may take some time to find it."

"There'll be plenty of time after school," suggested Samantha.

"There will be even more time if you don't go to school," pointed out Nanny Piggins.

Derrick and Michael smiled. As soon as Nanny Piggins had said they were walking to school, they knew they were unlikely to ever get there.

Nanny Piggins decided that the best way to find the truffle dump was to get a convertible car and drive around with her snout high in the air, trying to sniff it out. Fortunately, the retired army colonel who lived around the corner, and who was deeply in love with Nanny Piggins, owned a convertible. (He had bought it hoping to attract Nanny Piggins's admiration. And it had done just that. Unfortunately for the colonel, however, it had inspired Nanny Piggins's admiration for the car but not for him. At any rate, it took very little flirting before he offered to lend it to her.)

"Who is going to drive while I sniff?" asked Nanny Piggins.

"We can't drive! We're children!" exclaimed Samantha.

"Who better to drive than children?" argued Nanny Piggins. "Everybody knows children have better reflexes than adults, which is why they are so good at computer games. And children are much less likely to get into accidents because they don't spend half their time turning around to the backseat, telling children to behave."

"But children can't get driver's licenses," argued Derrick.

"Neither can pigs," said Nanny Piggins, "and I've never let a little thing like that stop me."

"Why don't I drive?" suggested Boris. "Because I'm a dancing bear, if I get stopped by the police, I can bamboozle them with some exotic footwork."

"Good thinking, Boris," said Nanny Piggins.

So Boris drove, which was not easy because he was ten feet tall, so his head stuck out three feet above the windshield, which meant that bugs kept getting squashed against his teeth and eyeballs. But Boris got along all right as long as he kept his eyes firmly closed and Michael told him which way to turn the wheel.

Meanwhile, Nanny Piggins held her snout high and sniffed, calling out instructions like "Smelly, smelly . . . smellier . . . really stinky . . . utterly foul!" as they got closer to unpleasant-smelling objects.

Really, the plan was going very well. The only problem was that Nanny Piggins's sense of smell was so acute, she kept sniffing out all foul-smelling things, not just truffles.

Their first stop was a drab suburban house.

"Is it here?" asked Derrick.

"There is definitely something odiously foul on these premises," said Nanny Piggins, her eyes watering as she tried to shield her snout from the unpleasant aroma.

Unfortunately, when they knocked on the door they found it was not truffles Nanny Piggins was smelling. The door was opened by Headmaster Pimplestock.

"What are you doing here?" demanded Nanny Piggins.

"What am I doing here?!" exclaimed Headmaster Pimplestock. "I live here. What are you doing here?"

"You live here! That explains the smell," said Nanny Piggins.

"The headmaster smells unbelievably foul?" asked Samantha.

Nanny Piggins sniffed at Headmaster Pimplestock's clothes. "It's hard to tell exactly where the smell comes from. I think there must be some kind of microscopic fungus growing on him that really stinks."

"How dare you!" yelled Headmaster Pimplestock. "Why aren't you three in school?"

"Why aren't you in school?" asked Nanny Piggins shrewdly.

The headmaster turned red in the face. "Uh...I'm unwell."

"You don't look unwell," said Nanny Piggins, peering around him and into his house. "Is that a toy train I can hear? You haven't pretended to be sick so you can stay home and play with your model railway, have you?"

Headmaster Pimplestock looked simultaneously embarrassed and angry. But all he did was yell "Go away!" and slam the door in their faces.

So Nanny Piggins, Boris, and the children got back in the car and continued sniffing. Her snout led them out of the city, through the suburbs, and into the countryside. They drove through valleys, over hills, and around lakes.

"Can your nose really smell something this far away?" asked Michael.

"Oh yes," said Nanny Piggins. "There was once a man in Denmark who didn't have a bath for three years. Eventually all the pigs of the world got together and wrote him a letter because we could all smell him."

"Did he take a bath?" asked Derrick.

"Not voluntarily," said Nanny Piggins. "A swarm of

angry pigs from Sweden crossed the border and pushed him into a lake."

"No way!" exclaimed Michael.

"Oh yes, which is why it is important to take a bath at least once a month. Because Swedish pigs have terrible tempers," said Nanny Piggins.

"She's right," said Boris. "I once got bitten by a Swedish pig just because I forgot to return a book he'd lent me."

"Stop the car!" screamed Nanny Piggins.

"Another ice-cream truck?" asked Boris.

"No, the smell. It is at its most foul," said Nanny Piggins. "What I would give to have another banana to shove up my snout right now."

"I've got an apple," volunteered Michael.

"No, thank you," said Nanny Piggins. "My snout is big, but not that big."

And so they all got out of the convertible and followed Nanny Piggins on foot as she sniffed her way across a field, down a hill, and into a gully.

"Urgh, it's so sickening. I almost feel like throwing up the eight jelly doughnuts I had for breakfast," said Nanny Piggins.

"You had twelve jelly doughnuts for breakfast," Samantha reminded her.

"I wouldn't throw them all up. I have to maintain my strength," said Nanny Piggins.

"So is the hole nearby?" asked Derrick.

"Yes. In fact, Michael, be careful, because if you took another step forward, you would plummet into the hole and meet certain death when you land on the enormous pile of truffles at the bottom," said Nanny Piggins.

Michael took a hasty step back. The others peered at the hole in front of him. It did not look like a hole because it had been boarded up. But the wooden boards were rotting with age. And now even the children could smell that there was something stinky deep within.

"Right," said Nanny Piggins, as she took a crowbar out of her handbag. She always carried a crowbar in case she had to borrow a cup of sugar from a neighbor and there was no one at home to let her in.

Nanny Piggins had soon levered up the wooden planks. And they all peered into the hole.

"It's an abandoned mine shaft," said Nanny Piggins. "I dumped the truffles in here because it saved me from having to dig a hole."

"I thought you liked digging holes," said Michael.

"I do," agreed Nanny Piggins. "But when you've got an armful of odorous truffles, you want to get them deep in the ground as quickly as possible."

So Nanny Piggins quickly rigged up some rappelling gear (which fortunately the colonel kept in the trunk of his car on the off chance Nanny Piggins agreed to elope with him). Then they all had an extremely animated debate about who would be lowered into the hole. Michael was eventually chosen because he had recently had a cold and still had a blocked nose, so the stench would affect him the least. Then Nanny Piggins strapped him in, and Boris lowered Michael into the hole.

At first the mine shaft just seemed to disappear into blackness. But as Michael slowly descended, the flashlight Nanny Piggins had sticky-taped to his head began to illuminate the bottom. He could not believe his eyes. The ground at the bottom of the mine shaft was not visible because it was covered with truffles. Ugly brown knobbly truffles were stacked everywhere three feet deep.

"Wow!" said Michael. Because it is hard to think of

clever things to say when you realize you are about to become incredibly rich.

A few hours later, Nanny Piggins and the children were dragging big garbage bags full of truffles into Pierre's restaurant. There were tears in the French chef's eyes as he smelled the ugly little lumps of fungus.

"*Sacre bleu!*" (which is French for "Gosh!") exclaimed Pierre. "This is an avalanche of truffles. With these I will be able to make the finest cordon bleu cuisine in the country." Pierre wrapped Nanny Piggins in a big hug. Then he started kissing Boris and the children repeatedly, on one cheek and then the other.

"Ahem," said Nanny Piggins, interrupting his joyous effusions. "There is the little matter of payment."

"Of course," said Pierre. "This huge amount of truffles is worth hundreds of thousands of dollars. And it will be worth every penny. Let me fetch my checkbook."

"Oh no," said Nanny Piggins, stopping him by grabbing his hand. "I think you can do a little better than that."

There were tears in the French chef's eyes as he smelled the ugly little lumps of fungus.

"Better than money?" said Pierre, looking confused. "What do you mean?"

"You're a chef, aren't you?" said Nanny Piggins. "Why would I take payment in the form of money when I could take payment in food?"

"You will give me all these truffles in exchange for a meal?" queried Pierre, wondering if the pig was crazy.

"We're hungry," explained Boris.

"We only had chocolate cookies for lunch," added Samantha.

"So don't you try to get out of it," threatened Nanny Piggins, "or we will take these truffles home and start flushing them down the toilet, which is what I really should have done with them in the first place."

"*Non, non, non,* don't do that," protested Pierre. "If it is a meal you want, I shall cook you a meal, the finest gourmet meal you have ever eaten. A meal worthy of the greatest snout in the world!"

Now you would think that the story ends here, with Nanny Piggins, Boris, and the children finishing their day by sitting down to enjoy a lovely gourmet meal. Unfortunately that is not quite how it went. You see, Nanny Piggins had eaten an enormous amount of food in her lifetime, and an enormous amount of what she considered delicious food—namely cake. But she had never actually eaten a gourmet meal. And let us just say that her disgust for the smell of truffles did not come close to matching her disgust for the size of Pierre's portions. Nanny Piggins did not like being short-changed when it came to food. And sadly, it is a strange fact of life that the finer and more expensive the restaurant, the smaller and tinier the food they serve you.

"What's this?" asked Nanny Piggins as Pierre set the first course in front of her.

"Your entrée. Vegetable confit," said Pierre.

"You mean this isn't the after-dinner mint?" asked Nanny Piggins.

"No," said Pierre.

"It's the size of an after-dinner mint," said Nanny Piggins.

"We don't serve after-dinner mints," said Pierre.

"I'm not surprised," said Nanny Piggins. "It would put the size of your portions to shame."

"What are you talking about?" said Pierre.

"I want to know why there is so little food on my plate," Nanny Piggins demanded loudly.

"This exquisite small dish is meant to stimulate the palate," protested Pierre.

"And why is it all stacked up? If you're only going to put half a mouthful on the plate, why don't you spread it out so I can see what I'm eating?" accused Nanny Piggins.

"*How dare you!*" yelled Pierre. "I am the finest chef for a thousand miles!"

"Chef?! Ha!!" yelled back Nanny Piggins. "Starvation organizer, that's what they should call you! How dare you serve these crumbs to us? These are growing children."

"*Ahem,*" said Boris, pretending to clear his throat.

"And this is a growing bear," added Nanny Piggins. "Do you want them to go to bed hungry?!"

And so Nanny Piggins and Pierre yelled at each other for a long time. She would have thrown the food at him, but it was not big enough to hurt him, so she did not bother. Pierre insisted that it was award-winning cuisine; Nanny Piggins insisted that it wouldn't satisfy a petite mouse.

In the end Nanny Piggins stormed out, Boris and the children followed her, and they enjoyed a lovely meal at the pizza joint next door.

"I'm sorry it didn't work out with the truffles," said Samantha. "Are you terribly disappointed you didn't sell them?"

"Not at all," said Nanny Piggins. "It is always better to accept food instead of money because you can't eat money. Well, you can, but it will make you very sick if you eat a lot of it. I had no way of knowing that Pierre was such a terrible chef."

"A lot of people think Pierre is a very good chef," Derrick pointed out.

"A lot of people will let an odorous, stinking truffle grow in their garden and not bother to dig it up and burn it. Which just goes to show how silly most people are," said Nanny Piggins.

And so Nanny Piggins, Boris, and the children enjoyed their pizza meal and returned home satisfied with their day's work. Sure, they had missed out on hundreds of thousands of dollars. But they had enjoyed a lovely day not going to school, and that was priceless.

CHAPTER NINE

Headmistress Piggins

Nanny Piggins and the children were crouched outside the dining room with their ears pressed to the door. They had been waiting there for a full eight minutes, but they could still hear the sound of Mr. Green chomping away at his high-fiber cereal.

"What's he doing?" asked Michael. "Why won't he go away?"

"He's usually been at the office for hours by now," said Derrick.

"We can't eat with him still in there," said Samantha. "We won't be able to digest our food." (Just being in the same room as Mr. Green had an unpleasant effect on his children's intestines.)

"He must be up to something," said Nanny Piggins.

"Perhaps his watch is broken," suggested Samantha.

"Perhaps he's gone insane," suggested Derrick.

"Or," said Nanny Piggins, "perhaps he wants to talk to us."

"Why?" asked Derrick, racking his brain trying to remember the last time his father had wanted to talk to him.

"I'm sure it could be any number of diabolical reasons. But there's only one way to find out. We'll have to go in," declared Nanny Piggins as she took hold of the doorknob.

"No!" shrieked Michael as he grabbed his nanny's hand. "Can't we go to school hungry instead?"

"Michael Green! How could you say such a thing?" admonished Nanny Piggins, genuinely horrified. "I will not allow anyone to go anywhere feeling hungry. I'd sooner hit your father over the head with a fruit bowl and drag his unconscious body out to the garden first."

"Is that your plan?" asked Derrick hopefully.

"Not exactly. I haven't been paid yet this month, so I'd rather avoid hitting him until after then," said Nanny Piggins. "Come on, children, brace yourselves."

And with that Nanny Piggins threw open the door and stepped into the dining room.

Fortunately Mr. Green wanted to eat breakfast with his children exactly as much as they wanted to eat breakfast with him. So they had barely entered the room before Mr. Green leaped from his seat and snatched up his briefcase.

"Ah, Nanny Piggins," he said while striding toward the doorway. "How lucky I should see you. I can't make the school's fund-raising dinner tonight. You'll have to go for me."

He almost made it out the door before completing this sentence, but not quite. Nanny Piggins stuck her leg out and tripped him. So instead of getting into his vomit-yellow Rolls-Royce and speeding away, Mr. Green lay sprawled on his dining room floor wondering what had happened.

"I'm sorry, Mr. Green. What was that you said?" asked Nanny Piggins, spreading marmalade on her toast as if she had not just brutally sent him to the floor.

Mr. Green got up, a little shaken, and turned to face his family. The children were eating quite happily now. While eating with their father took all the fun out of food, eating with their father sprawled on the floor made food taste twice as delicious.

"Er..." said Mr. Green.

"I understand that you want me to go to a dinner tonight," said Nanny Piggins. "But I don't understand how you intend to make it worth my while."

"For the pleasure of it?" began Mr. Green.

Nanny Piggins just shook her head.

"For the usual amount of chocolate mud cake?" suggested Mr. Green.

"Yes, I think that will do it," agreed Nanny Piggins. So after successfully blackmailing Mr. Green and finally allowing him to go to work, Nanny Piggins turned to the children to find out just what she had agreed to.

"Headmaster Pimplestock organizes this dinner every year," explained Derrick. "You pay ten times what it's worth for a plate of overcooked chicken."

"Then during dessert, when you've finally got something decent to eat, they distract you by auctioning off things nobody wants," added Samantha.

"But everybody bids because they're bored and they want to be allowed to go home," concluded Michael.

"And it's legal to subject parents to substandard food and force them to buy things they don't want?" asked Nanny Piggins.

"Oh yes," said Samantha. "Schools do it all the time."

"I can see I should have asked Mr. Green to give me twice as much cake as usual," said Nanny Piggins. "Oh well. I'm sure I'll find some way to amuse myself once I'm there."

And she did. Nanny Piggins was very good at amusing herself in otherwise unpleasant circumstances. For a start, she took Boris with her. It was normal to take your husband or wife, and since Nanny Piggins did not have either, she thought her brother would do. It is amazing how taking along a ten-foot dancing bear always manages to cheer up a situation. Especially when he is dressed for dancing in his very best black tie.

Headmaster Pimplestock was greeting all the parents at the door. He looked nervous when he saw Nanny Piggins. Even though she was only four feet tall, she scared him. It had something to do with her piercing brown eyes and the fact that she kept ringing up and threatening him every time the children were sent home with math homework. But when he saw Boris, a looming giant of a bear, that was too much. The headmaster looked like he was going to faint.

"Er, I'm afraid, Miss Piggins, that pets are not allowed at the dinner," said Headmaster Pimplestock.

"I should think not," said Nanny Piggins. "It would be cruelty to animals to subject them to substandard food and boring speeches. If you did let pets in, I'd have to report you to the ASPCA."

"I'm referring to your..." The headmaster tried to indicate Boris without actually pointing.

"My what?" asked Nanny Piggins.

"Your b-e-a-r," spelled out Headmaster Pimplestock.

"I'm not one of your students, so I absolutely refuse to take part in a spelling test," declared Nanny Piggins.

"Your bear, we can't let in your bear," whispered the headmaster.

"He's not my bear," said Nanny Piggins loudly. "He is my brother. And he's a lot cleaner and more hygienic than the humans you let in. I saw the state of your science teacher's fingernails." (All the conversation in the hall fell silent as everyone in the room followed Nanny Piggins's outstretched trotter to see exactly which science teacher she meant. And poor Mr. Sims made it doubly clear by trying to hide his hands behind his back.) "How dare you cast aspersions on my brother when your own humans are not up to scratch? Come along, Boris."

Nanny Piggins and Boris strode into the hall, and the headmaster, realizing there was absolutely nothing he could do about it, decided to pretend that the conversation had never happened.

Derrick, Samantha, and Michael were all at the dinner too. Children were being used by the school as waiters and dishwashers to save money (and violate child labor laws). So Nanny Piggins was able to get the children to point out their more unpleasant teachers.

She made Derrick identify his geography teacher, Mr. Doyle. Just the previous week, Mr. Doyle had "accidentally" spilled coffee on Derrick's diorama of a volcano and given him a D when it failed to erupt. As soon as Nanny Piggins knew who he was, she crawled under the tables to bite his leg. Actually, she bit the leg of the woman sitting next to him first. But that was Mrs. Doyle and she was just as unpleasant as her husband, so it did not matter.

Then Nanny Piggins made Samantha point out her art teacher, Mrs. Anderson. Mrs. Anderson had made Samantha cry the previous week when she said her still life painting of a banana lacked imagination. The truth was that it did lack imagination. Samantha knew that and Nanny Piggins knew that. But in Nanny Piggins's opinion, a teacher should have the sensitivity not to say such mean things, however true, in front of the entire class. So Nanny Piggins snuck across the room and emptied a jar of worms into Mrs. Anderson's handbag.

The children were right in their prediction: The food was inedible chicken. Fortunately Nanny Piggins had brought a large chocolate cake in her handbag, so she and Boris did not have to eat the overcooked chicken Kiev. Instead they used the rubbery meat as cushions because the chairs in the hall were of that unusually hard and uncomfortable plastic variety that schools always seem to prefer.

Nanny Piggins and Boris whiled away the time trying to pick out the most bored parent. Nanny Piggins saw a man who looked like he was about to slip into a coma. But Boris had the advantage of being taller, and he spotted a woman down the back of the hall who had actually fallen asleep, her cheek slumped in her coleslaw.

Finally the plates were cleared away and dessert was brought out. Samantha placed two plates of wafer-thin brown stuff in front of Nanny Piggins and Boris.

"What's that?" asked Nanny Piggins.

Samantha hesitated and then, in an ashamed voice, admitted, "Chocolate cake."

"It is?" asked Boris. "How can you tell? There's so little of it."

"Why is it such an atomically small portion? I practically need an electron microscope to see what I'm eating. They're not trying to make us lose weight, are they?" demanded Nanny Piggins. "Because if they are, I will leave right now!"

"No, they are small portions because Headmaster Pimplestock is incredibly cheap," said Samantha, blushing, because it always embarrassed her to be critical, even when she was being strictly accurate. "He bought just one chocolate cake to feed three hundred parents."

"He did what?!" exclaimed Nanny Piggins. "We should call the police!"

"That's just wrong," agreed Boris.

"Sharing a cake between three hundred people—that's the most barbaric type of crime there is!" declared Nanny Piggins, leaping up to make a citizen's arrest.

"Shh," pleaded Samantha, grabbing hold of her nanny's arm. "If you get the headmaster thrown in jail, he's sure to give us all bad report cards."

"It'll be worth it," insisted Nanny Piggins.

"No, it won't," said Samantha. "You know Father docks your pay if we get bad grades. And no money means no chocolate."

"All right," conceded Nanny Piggins, reluctantly sitting back on her chicken Kiev. "I'll let it slide this time. But I'm only restraining myself for your sake, because chocolate is such a vitally important part of every child's diet."

The auction was even more boring than the chicken dinner. Nanny Piggins had absolutely no interest in bidding for ukulele lessons or dinner for two at the dingiest Italian restaurant in town. So she was under the tables again, crawling across the room to bite Michael's English teacher, when the auctioneer called out the final item for the night. "Headmaster for a day! Who would like to be headmaster for a day?"

Now it just so happened that at this exact same moment Headmaster Pimplestock was patting his pockets, saying, "I appear to have lost fifty dollars. I must have dropped it." (I do not want to accuse the headmaster of stealing the leftover chocolate cake budget. But it is quite the coincidence — such a small cake and so much cash in his pocket.)

Meanwhile, Nanny Piggins was on her hands and knees under the headmaster's table and she saw a crumpled piece of paper on the floor in front of her. She immediately recognized it as her favorite type of paper — money. She scooped it up and leaped out from under the table, yelling, "Fifty dollars!"

"Sold to the pig with the fifty-dollar bill!" cried the auctioneer.

"Sold to the pig with the fifty-dollar bill!"
cried the auctioneer.

And that is how Nanny Piggins accidentally bought a day as the school's headmaster.

She did not cry when the auctioneer took the banknote out of her hand, although she really did want to. She could not understand what was happening. Why would anyone want to be headmaster for the day? Indeed, that was precisely the problem. None of the parents wanted to, and none of them showed any interest in bidding on it, which was why the auctioneer was so quick to snap up Nanny Piggins's bid.

Nanny Piggins, Boris, and the children walked home feeling glum. They were all lost in their own thoughts.

"What a waste of fifty dollars," said Nanny Piggins.

"What a horrible thing to do to a chicken," said Boris.

"Thank you for biting Mr. Doyle," said Derrick.

"It's going to be fun having you as our headmaster," said Michael.

"I don't think so," said Nanny Piggins. "I'm not looking forward to growing a beard and wearing ugly clothes."

"But that's not all that headmasters do," said Samantha.

"It's not?" asked Nanny Piggins.

"No, they set all the rules in the school. They are in

charge of all the teachers and they decide what the students are going to study," explained Derrick.

"Really?" said Nanny Piggins. She was beginning to get interested. "Hmm, this might not be so bad after all. I definitely don't have to grow a beard?"

"Not unless you want to," Samantha assured her.

And so, on Monday morning, Nanny Piggins accompanied Derrick, Samantha, and Michael to school. Boris went along as well because he did not want to get lonely at home. Headmaster Pimplestock greeted Nanny Piggins at the gates. He opened his mouth to say something about Boris but then closed it again, deciding perhaps he had better not.

"Welcome to the school, Miss Piggins," called the headmaster.

"Headmistress Piggins, you mean," corrected Nanny Piggins.

Headmaster Pimplestock laughed. "Yes, yes, Headmistress Piggins. We're going to start the day with an assembly where you can address the school."

"No, we're not. I'm the headmistress, and I can't think of anything more stupid than getting five hundred children in a room and boring them," said Nanny Piggins.

"That's what we do every Monday morning," protested the headmaster.

"Not now that I'm headmistress," declared Nanny Piggins.

"You do, er...realize that you're not actually headmistress. 'Headmistress for the day' is more an honorary, symbolic title," said Headmaster Pimplestock.

"I paid fifty dollars—that's eight chocolate cakes' worth of money—to be headmistress and I intend to be headmistress," declared Nanny Piggins, drawing herself up to the full four feet of her height.

"I can't allow anarchy to..." began the headmaster.

But Nanny Piggins interrupted. "Throw him off the grounds, Boris. I don't even know what he's doing here. He doesn't have a job anymore."

"You do realize your position is just for one day?" squealed Headmaster Pimplestock as Boris picked him up and carried him to the far side of the gate.

"You can get a lot done in one day if you set your

mind to it," said Nanny Piggins mysteriously. "Now hurry along, children, you'd better get to class. I have things to do."

The first thing Nanny Piggins did was fire the entire math department. She was very nice about it. She assured the math teachers she did not hold it against them personally. They had obviously all suffered some terrible trauma in early life for them to go into such a cruel profession. But in her opinion any math beyond the ability to calculate the cost of a mixed bag of candy was a waste of time. (Plus, she knew they would easily get jobs elsewhere. No doubt something involving taxes because of all their experience with numbers and misery.) She replaced the math teachers with a staff of chefs to teach the children how to cook, saying, "We all eat three meals a day, sometimes more, whereas you can go your whole life without ever doing quadratic equations."

She then lined the whole school up along the soccer field, gave every child a ball, and got them to throw the balls at the gym teachers, to see how much they liked dodgeball. There was some squealing and many, many red welts. But the sports teachers soon got the message about bullying not being all right just because you are wearing a whistle.

After that, Nanny Piggins bulldozed the school cafeteria, explaining that it was wrong to allow the site of such crimes against food to continue to exist.

Then she sent all the children home to get changed. (Now, you might think that having been told to go home, the children would not come back. But they all did because they knew what was going to come next.) Nanny Piggins forced all the teachers to wear uniforms. Pink uniforms, because pink looks good on pigs, so why not on teachers? Some of the teachers complained. But as Nanny Piggins pointed out, "If you like uniforms so much, why shouldn't you wear them?" And it made more sense for children to wear regular clothes and teachers uniforms because "children have a better dress sense than teachers, as far as I can see."

In short, by lunchtime (a meal entirely consisting of chocolate), the whole student body loved Headmistress Piggins. There were cheers of joy and gratitude everywhere she went on the school grounds.

The staff, on the other hand, were not so comfortable. After lunch the secretarial staff met Nanny Piggins in the headmaster's office in tears.

"What's wrong?" asked Nanny Piggins. "Surely you don't want that boring old headmaster back?"

"No, not at all," said the most senior secretary. "He never let us order chocolate cookies. And you've given us a packet each on your first day. So we're loyal to you to the end. But we're concerned. The district superintendent is due to inspect the school at two o'clock this afternoon, and we're worried you'll get in trouble."

"If this superintendent really is as super as his job title implies, then I don't see how he can be upset with me when I've made so many excellent improvements," said Nanny Piggins.

"But if the superintendent is unhappy, he won't just take it out on you," said the senior secretary. "He can withhold funding for the school physics excursion."

"What's so good about a physics excursion?" asked Nanny Piggins.

"All the children get to go to an amusement park and go on the rides to observe centrifugal force and gravity," said the senior secretary.

"Do the students really do that?" asked Nanny Piggins suspiciously.

"No, they eat too much junk food and go on the rides until they're sick," explained the secretary.

"Then they cannot be allowed to miss out on such a valuable learning experience," declared Nanny Piggins. "Don't worry. I'll deal with this super person."

Fortunately, impressing the district superintendent was a lot easier than Nanny Piggins had imagined. He was a plump elderly man who led a quiet life, never having married. But as soon as he saw Nanny Piggins, he fell in love. He had always been attracted to short women with peaches-and-cream complexions. It never occurred to him that his perfect woman was a pig until he saw Nanny Piggins.

But it was not just Nanny Piggins's appearance that won him over. He also fell in love with her educational theories. He approved of her decision to take all the school's required English texts and run them through a wood chipper. Both because the pages provided excellent mulch for the school gardens and because she allowed the children to read books they might actually enjoy, having formed the radical theory that if children were allowed to enjoy reading, they were likely to read more.

The superintendent was equally delighted by Nanny Piggins's approach to geography. She got the children to make prank calls to foreign countries. If you really want to know the chief imports and exports of Istanbul (not that Nanny Piggins could see why you would), the best way to find out was to ring someone in Istanbul. And, as an added bonus, if you ring them up at three o'clock in the morning their time, you will learn some interesting local colloquialisms.

"Brilliant!" exclaimed the superintendent.

And when Nanny Piggins taught a history class by regaling the children with colorful (naughty) stories from her own life, he thought it was a wonderful example of oral history in action.

So by the time he had finished his inspection, the superintendent was convinced Nanny Piggins was the best headmistress he had ever seen (and he secretly wanted to marry her).

"Headmistress Piggins," said the district superintendent. "I must insist you leave this job immediately."

"But I thought you liked the work I was doing here," protested Nanny Piggins.

"I do. That's why I want you to leave and join head office. You must institute your brilliant educational theories across the entire school district, then the country. And then, I believe, we should make it our mission to spread your ideas across the entire world," gushed the superintendent.

"No," declared Nanny Piggins.

"No?" asked the superintendent, trying not to cry.

"While it is a tempting offer and, goodness knows, schools are the silliest institutions, I'm afraid I'd rather not," said Nanny Piggins.

"Why not?" asked the superintendent.

"I already have a job," said Nanny Piggins. "I'm a nanny. And there is no more important job than that. The three children in my care may grow up to be astronauts, presidents, or semiamateur jugglers. And it's my job to make sure they do whichever one suits them best."

"But the education system needs you," pleaded the superintendent.

"Yes, I know, because schools are cruel, illogical, and unfair. But the thing is, life is cruel, illogical, and unfair.

That is why the education system works so well. If schools and teachers did a good job and inspired children and made them enthusiastic about every subject, they would only be sadly disappointed when they got out into the real world. Better to disappoint them when they're young. It is more important to learn to cope with disappointment than learn how to do long division."

"You are a very wise pig, Miss Piggins," said the superintendent.

"True," said Nanny Piggins.

"If you won't come and work with me to improve the standard of schools, can you at least do me one favor?" asked the superintendent.

"What's that?" asked Nanny Piggins.

"Will you allow me to have one kiss?" asked the superintendent, leaning toward her cheek.

"No," declared Nanny Piggins, putting up her trotter to block the path of his lips.

"No?" said the superintendent, feeling rather crushed.

"I can see you are already in love with me. It is a common effect I have on men. Maybe one day, years from now, you will get over it enough to settle down with another woman. But if I let you have one kiss—no other woman will ever live up to me and you will be sad and lonely for life. So it is for your own good that we shall just shake hands," said Nanny Piggins.

"Thank you, Nanny Piggins," said the superintendent, taking her trotter in his hand. "It has been an honor and a privilege, and I shall never wash my hand again."

"That is a lovely, if disgustingly unhygienic, compliment, so I thank you," said Nanny Piggins.

And so, in just one short day, Nanny Piggins became the most successful headmistress of all time, and then retired so as not to disturb the educational system of the entire world. This made Derrick, Samantha, and Michael happy because, while they loved her as a headmistress, they really, really loved her as their nanny.

CHAPTER TEN

Nanny Piggins Delivers Justice

Nanny Piggins and the children were playing Hairdressers, which sounds like a perfectly nice, civilized game. But not the way Nanny Piggins played it. She had learned her hairdressing technique from a Bhutanese warrior princess (the men in her kingdom never liked getting haircuts). So this game of Hairdressers involved crawling under hedges, around garbage bins, and over fences as they stalked their prey—the postman. When they caught him, they would whip out the clippers and attack. I know it seems aggressive, but the postman did not mind, because they always gave him a fashionable haircut. Plus Nanny Piggins always gave him a cup of tea and a slice of cake before they sent him on his way again. Indeed, since Nanny Piggins moved into the neighborhood, the postman had saved a fortune on going to the barber.

On this particular morning, Nanny Piggins and the children were distracted from their grooming task. Just as they were about to swoop on the postman, pull him off his bicycle, tie him up, and start snipping, they saw him deliver a letter into their very own mailbox. Nanny Piggins was torn—she did enjoy giving the postman a haircut (she was going to give him a flattop this month), but she was also burning with curiosity about the letter. So she called together her Bhutanese warriors (just in time, because Michael was about to drop onto the postman from out of a tree), and they ran over to look at the mail.

Nanny Piggins's curiosity was rewarded because there was one letter addressed to her. It was obviously very important because it was typewritten and did not smell of animal droppings (which is what all the letters

Nanny Piggins received from her circus friends always smelled like).

"Open it," suggested Derrick.

"What if it's booby-trapped?" asked Nanny Piggins.

"Who would send you a booby-trapped letter?" worried Samantha.

"A very long list of people," admitted Nanny Piggins.

"I know!" said Michael. "Let's trick Father into opening it for you."

"That wouldn't be very fair. What if there is a venomous snake or an ancient Egyptian curse inside?" said Nanny Piggins. Then she thought about how, only that morning, Mr. Green had forbidden her from holding a tango marathon in his living room, and she changed her mind. "Let's do it!"

They rushed inside. Mr. Green just happened to be at the house that morning because the office building where he worked was being fumigated. The building had a terrible infestation of cockroaches, which had spread from Mr. Green's very own desk, because he ate all his meals there and he never cleaned up properly.

So Mr. Green was sitting in the living room reading the newspaper and desperately trying to ignore the existence of his children. He did not even look up when Nanny Piggins handed him the letter. He just grunted, and, without taking his eyes off the paper, he started opening it. Nanny Piggins and the children took cover behind the couch with their fingers in their ears, just in case. But when Mr. Green tore the envelope open, there was no explosion or wild animal jumping out. Mr. Green did not even shrivel up in a puff of green smoke. He simply slipped out some folded sheets of paper.

"Thank you," said Nanny Piggins, snatching them out of his hand and running out of the room. Upstairs, in the safety of her bedroom, Nanny Piggins and the children looked at the letter. The letterhead said it was from the government. Nanny Piggins hid her head under the quilt because she was afraid to read any more. She had always worried about what would happen if the government found out about any one of the number of technically not quite legal things she did on a daily basis. So Samantha kept reading for her.

"It says that you, Sarah Piggins, are required to report for jury duty," read Samantha.

"Jury duty? What on earth is that?" asked Nanny Piggins.

"When they have court cases, they get twelve people to come in to decide whether or not the person is guilty," explained Derrick.

"You mean I'll get to decide whether to send someone to jail?" asked Nanny Piggins excitedly.

"Yes," said Derrick.

"That's easy," said Nanny Piggins. "I'll just write a letter now saying that they're innocent."

"But you don't know what the crime is or who's standing trial yet," protested Samantha.

"But I'm sure even if they did it, they didn't mean to," said Nanny Piggins. "I break rules all the time and I never mean to get caught."

"That's not how a jury works," said Derrick. "You have to go to the trial and listen to everything all the lawyers have to say."

"I don't know about this," said Nanny Piggins. "It sounds awfully like work."

"You don't have any choice," said Samantha. "You've been summonsed."

"I've been whatsied?" asked Nanny Piggins.

"It means you've been officially told you have to go by the government," said Samantha.

"Really?" said Nanny Piggins, beginning to look very mutinous. "I have to, do I?"

"They'll give you free sandwiches for lunch," said Derrick, hastily trying to defuse the situation.

"Oh, well, that's all right, then. They really should put that in the letter," said Nanny Piggins, suddenly cheering up. "Let's go."

And so Nanny Piggins and the children reported for jury duty. The children should have been at school, but Nanny Piggins thought it was important they learn about the legal system. And the children thought it was important to go with Nanny Piggins, just in case she tried to run away. They did not want their nanny getting in trouble. When they arrived at the court-house, Nanny Piggins and the children were put in a room with a large number of very dreary-looking people.

"Why does everyone look so sad?" asked Nanny Piggins. "They're not the ones going to jail, are they?"

"No, they're the other jurors," explained Derrick. "They're just sad that they couldn't think of an excuse to get out of it."

"But why would they want to get out of jury duty?" asked Nanny Piggins. "I've seen what most people do with their time, and it's a lot more boring than sending criminals to jail."

"I think people like being boring," said Samantha.

"Your father certainly does," agreed Nanny Piggins.

"Here comes the judge," whispered Derrick. "He'll help select the jury."

Everyone in the courtroom had to stand up as an elderly, grumpy-looking man wearing a black gown entered. This caused a lot of consternation among the Green children because they all had to shove their handkerchiefs in Nanny Piggins's mouth to muffle her loud exclamation, "Why is that man wearing a dress?!"

When the old dress-wearing man sat down, they could all sit down too. He then began the process of jury selection, which immediately bored Nanny

Piggins, so she took out a pack of cards and played canasta with the children. That was, until her own name was called. "Sarah Matahari Lorelai Piggins."

"Yes," said Nanny Piggins, getting to her feet.

"You are on the jury," said the judge.

"All right," said Nanny Piggins as she slipped out of her seat and walked to the front of the courtroom.

"Hang on!" called the defense counsel. "You can't put her on the jury."

"Why not?" demanded the judge grumpily. He did not like being told what he could and could not do.

"She's a—" The defense counsel looked across at Nanny Piggins. Nanny Piggins glared back at him. "A pig," he whispered uncomfortably.

"What?" asked the judge, who was hard of hearing.

"A pig, Your Honor. A porker. A farm animal. The type of creature bacon comes from," expanded the defense counsel.

Nanny Piggins was really glaring at him now. If they did not find the defendant guilty in this trial, there was a good chance Nanny Piggins would be found guilty of biting this defense counsel.

The judge lowered his reading glasses and took a

good look at Nanny Piggins. There was no doubt that, no matter how well dressed and stunningly beautiful she was, Nanny Piggins clearly was a pig. But the judge did not like the defense counsel. And he did not much like being a judge. So he decided to make things interesting for himself by allowing a pig on the jury.

"I don't see why Miss Piggins's species should be held against her," said the judge.

Nanny Piggins took an immediate liking to the judge.

"But Your Honor," spluttered the counsel, "you can't put my client's fate in the hands of a pig."

"The trotters of a pig, you mean," corrected the judge.

"Surely it's against the rules," protested the counsel.

"According to the law, your client is entitled to a jury of his peers," said the judge. "And he is, after all, undeniably a porker."

The defense counsel looked at his client. There was no way around it. He had a weight problem.

"I've made my decision and that is final," said the judge.

"Thank you, Your Honor." Nanny Piggins smiled graciously before turning around, pointing dramatically at the defendant, and yelling, "I find him *guilty*!"

"Not yet, Miss Piggins," said the judge. "It is

traditional to listen to the evidence before making your verdict."

"Oh, all right, if that's the way it's done," said Nanny Piggins.

"Why don't you take a seat in the jury box?" suggested the judge.

"Thank you. Come along, children," said Nanny Piggins.

Derrick, Samantha, and Michael hopped up from their seats at the back of the courtroom and went to join Nanny Piggins in the jury box.

"Your Honor, you can't allow children to sit with the jury!" protested the defense counsel.

"Can't I?" growled the judge, who did not like being told what he could and could not do by pimply lawyers still in their twenties.

"I'm a nanny. I have to take them everywhere with me. It's my job," said Nanny Piggins.

"You heard the pig," said the judge.

"If I left them at home unattended, they might burn the house down. Then I'd be brought in on trial for neglecting them," explained Nanny Piggins.

"And we don't want that, do we?" said the judge,

glaring at the defense counsel. "We've got quite enough to do without trying Nanny Piggins."

"Yes, Your Honor," said the defense counsel humbly, realizing he was not going to get his way on anything.

And so the trial began. Nanny Piggins found it quite thrilling. She got in trouble several times for leaping up and yelling "Guilty!" as well as "You should be ashamed of yourself!" and "You are going to rot in jail for a very long time!" (and that was just what she said to the defense counsel). But the judge was very halfhearted with his tellings-off because he enjoyed the interruptions.

You see, the truth is, court cases are very boring and not at all like they are on television. So having a pig unexpectedly yelling things out all the time really cheered the proceedings up. The court stenographer kept making typing mistakes because she was giggling so hard. And she had no idea how to spell *wastrel, popinjay, cabbage head*, or some of the other insults Nanny Piggins kept hurling at the defendant and his counsel. Meanwhile, the public prosecutor practically bit through the handle of his briefcase, he was struggling so hard not to laugh.

It took all day for the lawyers to lay out the details of the case, even though they were pretty straightforward.

The defendant was accused of shinnying up a drainpipe, taking two tiles out of the roof, squeezing into the attic, climbing down into the house, and stealing an old lady's purebred Siamese cat. Which, according to an expert witness, was very valuable because it was an unusually high-strung breed that never showed affection for anyone unless they had a tin of cat food in their hand.

The defendant had been caught with the stolen cat locked in his bedroom wardrobe, which did look pretty incriminating. But his counsel was maintaining a spirited defense based largely on the improbability of such an obviously overweight man committing such an athletically demanding crime. Also, his client was allergic to cats.

In conclusion, the prosecutor, followed by the defense counsel, summed up their cases for the jury. The defense counsel seemed quite willing to talk into the night and on into the next day. But the judge had caught something of Nanny Piggins's spirit for spontaneous interjection. So whenever the defense counsel started getting unnecessarily wordy, the judge would mutter, "Get on with it" or "Hush your cake hole."

Finally it was over, and the judge turned to the jury to give them his instructions. "Members of the jury, first you need to choose a foreperson. Then you must reach a verdict. If you think he is guilty, then your decision should be 'guilty.' If you think he's innocent, then your decision should be 'not guilty.' Take your time. I know decisions are hard. It always takes me ages to decide what to have for lunch."

And so the jury plus the three Green children were ushered into a room and left to get on with it. The jury immediately elected Nanny Piggins as their fore-pig. She had become very popular during the trial because she kept handing around a large voluminous handbag that contained cookies, cake, chocolate, and other essential provisions for sustaining themselves. Indeed, if it were not for Nanny Piggins, several of the jurors would have slept through most of the proceedings.

The jurors discussed the trial, which they all enjoyed because it was a lot like gossiping. They discussed the defense counsel's terrible dress sense. (Nanny Piggins had distinctly noticed he was wearing brown shoes with a black suit.) They discussed who was dreamier — the bailiff or the man who brought them their lunches. And they discussed whether the stenographer was really writing down everything that was said or just randomly pressing buttons on her typewriter and hoping nobody would notice. So by the end of the day, while they had talked through some very important matters, they had not reached a verdict. But the judge was very nice about it. He said they could come back the next day and not to rush.

And so the next day the jurors were put in their room again, and again they discussed the important points of the trial, and again they did not reach a decision. This went on for an entire week. Nanny Piggins was beginning to feel the pressure of being the fore-pig of the jury.

"I don't know what is wrong with them," Nanny Piggins confessed to the children. "They seem totally unable to make up their minds. Every day five of them think he's guilty, five of them think he's innocent, and one person is undecided."

"Couldn't you persuade them to agree with your opinion?" suggested Derrick. "That's what they always do in movies. One clever juror convinces all the other jurors that the verdict that is so obviously right is actually secretly wrong."

"I would do that," said Nanny Piggins, "because I do enjoy arguing with people and telling them they are wrong. But the problem is that the ones who think he's guilty and the ones who think he's innocent change every day. It's almost like they are randomly changing their opinions for no apparent reason."

"You could put them in a headlock and force them to agree with you," suggested Michael.

"I did consider that," agreed Nanny Piggins, "but they gave me a leaflet on what a fore-pig is meant to do and it specifically said *no headlocks*."

"What a shame," said Michael. He would like to have seen all eleven other members of the jury in a wrestling match with Nanny Piggins. He had no doubt she would win.

"We'll just have to continue our discussions," said Nanny Piggins as she pushed on the jury room door. But surprisingly, the door did not open because another juror was leaning on it. Nanny Piggins was just about to kick it open with a spinning sidekick when she caught what the juror was saying. "Who's going to pretend to think he's innocent and who's going to pretend to think he's guilty today?"

"I'll take innocent today," said Penelope the yoga instructor. "I've been arguing he's guilty for two days.

I've got some new ideas on why I can think he's innocent. I'm going to pretend I had a dream telling me how to vote."

"I'm going to pretend I think he's guilty because I'm angry with the world about never getting into art school," said Nick the data-entry clerk.

"Ooh, nice. I'm sure Nanny Piggins will fall for that one," the other jurors agreed.

Nanny Piggins had heard enough. She launched her spinning sidekick, knocking down the door and the juror leaning against it. "I've been listening in on everything you've been saying, and I am sadly disappointed!" declared Nanny Piggins. "How dare you lie to me, your fore-pig!"

The other jurors looked down with shame.

"Yes, you should all look at your shoes. Apart from the fact that you have every reason to be ashamed, several of you should acquaint yourselves with boot polish. And you, Susan, should really rethink sandals with that outfit. Now, why on earth are you pretending to have different verdicts?" asked Nanny Piggins.

The jurors looked sheepish. Finally Brian the accountant spoke up. "Because we like your cake so much."

"I beg your pardon?" asked Nanny Piggins.

"Every day you bring in cake," explained Georgina the pediatric nurse, "and it's mouthwateringly delicious. We don't want this trial to end because then we'll never eat your delicious cake again."

"And you all feel this way?" asked Nanny Piggins.

All the jurors nodded.

"Well, that's the loveliest perversion of justice anyone has ever committed for me," said Nanny Piggins, getting quite teary-eyed.

"Your cakes are amazing. Just when we think you've surpassed yourself with a mouthwatering chocolate mud cake, or a scintillatingly sticky date cake, you mix it up with a refreshing lemon drizzle cake. I go home at night and dream about what sort of cake you'll bake next," confessed Penelope the yoga instructor.

"Now you're making me blush," said Nanny Piggins.

"What sort of cake did you bring today?" asked Tim the piano tuner.

"Angel food cake with toffee sauce," revealed Nanny Piggins.

"Will you marry me?!" exclaimed Bert the nuclear physicist.

"Bert, you're already married," chided Nanny Piggins.

"I'm sure my wife won't mind, if you let her eat the cakes too," promised Bert.

"Much as I do enjoy baking you cakes every day, we probably should come to a verdict about this trial," said Nanny Piggins.

"Aww, do we have to?" pleaded the rest of the jury.

"Couldn't we drag it out for another fortnight?" begged Georgina. "You were talking about your caramel fudge cake the other day and I'm dying to try it."

"That is an extremely good cake," Michael agreed.

"We don't have to be here in the jury room to eat my cake," said Nanny Piggins.

"We don't?" said the jurors.

"No. If you want a slice of cake, just come over to our house. We have cake every day," said Nanny Piggins.

"Several times a day," added Samantha.

"That would work," agreed the jury.

"I guess we could come up with a verdict," said Bert reluctantly. "So that was a definite no on the marriage proposal, then?"

"A definite no, Bert," said Nanny Piggins sternly. "Now let's have a proper vote. Who thinks he's guilty?"

No one except Nanny Piggins put up their hand.

"Who thinks he's innocent?" asked Nanny Piggins.

No one at all put up their hand.

"How can you all think he's not innocent and not guilty?" asked Nanny Piggins.

"We think he looks guilty," said Aileen the stay-at-home housewife.

"His eyes are shifty," agreed Elliott the television repairman.

"And I don't like the way he combs his hair," said Georgina. "There's something untrustworthy about his parting."

"But we don't see how someone that fat could climb up a drainpipe, wriggle in through a hole in the roof, and squeeze out through the tiny laundry window," said Bert.

"Plus he is allergic to cats," Amy the receptionist reminded them.

"Is that all?" said Nanny Piggins. "I can show you how he did that. Never underestimate the agility and athleticism of a fat person. Over the years I have known many overweight pigs. Sadly it is a health issue that blights our species. And these 'big-boned' pigs have done extraordinarily athletic things, usually in the pursuit of more food. Why, my own mother once leaped from a moving truck, did a commando roll into an azalea bush, and squeezed in through a half-open window after smelling a freshly baked tart in the oven."

"That's amazing!" exclaimed Tim the piano tuner.

"I know," said Nanny Piggins. "It was a custard tart, so it was more than worth the effort."

"But really, Nanny Piggins," said Aileen the housewife, "surely a fat man like that could never climb up a drainpipe, in through a hole in the roof, and out through a laundry window carrying a cat cage."

"I know he could, and I can prove it," declared Nanny Piggins. "Derrick, run along home and fetch Boris. The rest of you, join me outside."

Five minutes later the jurors had all assembled outside in the parking lot. "Here they come," said Nanny Piggins, as she spotted Derrick and Boris loping up the street. "Now, the defendant weighs two hundred and seventy-six pounds."

"How do you know that?" interrupted Bert the nuclear physicist. "It wasn't in the evidence."

"I used to work in a circus," explained Nanny Piggins. "Circus folk just know these things."

The jurors mumbled their agreement.

"Now, this is my brother, Boris," said Nanny Piggins.

"Hello," said the jurors.

"Hello," said Boris.

"And Boris weighs—"

"Ahem," Boris interrupted, and cleared his throat. Nanny Piggins saw that he was feeling shy.

"A little bit more than the defendant. Although he has superior bone structure, so it suits him much better," added Nanny Piggins quickly.

Boris smiled.

"To demonstrate my point, Boris will now climb up the outside of the courthouse, remove two tiles from the roof, and climb in through the hole," said Nanny Piggins.

Everyone turned and looked at Boris expectantly.

"I don't know if I can do that," protested Boris.

"I've hidden a jar of honey in the roof," said Nanny Piggins.

Before she had even finished the sentence, Boris had taken off, scampering up the drainpipe, and was tearing tiles off the roof. The jurors watched in astonishment. They thought there was no way a thousand-pound, ten-foot-tall bear could get in through a hole the size of two roof tiles. But they were soon to be amazed. By jiggling, wiggling, bending, and stretching, Boris had squeezed his way in through the hole in under three seconds. After all, Boris was a Russian ballet dancer, so his flexibility was astounding. Then the jury knew he had found the jar of honey because they could hear the slurping and licking from down on the street.

"I think I have made my point," said Nanny Piggins.

"He's guilty as sin!" exclaimed Amy.

"Exactly," said Nanny Piggins.

"But what about his allergy to cats?" reminded Samantha.

"How could he possibly have stolen a cat if he has an allergy to cats?" asked Bert.

Nanny Piggins thought about this for a moment. Then her eyes began to shine. "I know!" She opened her large handbag and rummaged around for several minutes, setting aside breath mints, chocolate bars,

After all, Boris was a Russian ballet dancer,
so his flexibility was astounding.

maps to all the major cities of the world, a jar of worms, a crowbar . . . until she finally found what she was looking for—a clean and neatly folded handkerchief. "By using one of these!"

"A handkerchief! Of course!" exclaimed Georgina.

"Using a handkerchief, he could have simply blown his nose every time he wanted to sneeze. And still had a hand free to carry the cat cage," said Nanny Piggins. "The handkerchief is one of the most useful tools of the hardened criminal."

And so the jury returned to the courtroom and gave their verdict. They found the defendant guilty. (So, as it turned out, they would have saved a lot of time and money if they had just taken Nanny Piggins's word for it when she declared him guilty back at the beginning.)

And the jury could rest assured that they had made the right decision. Because as soon as they returned their verdict, the defendant leaped athletically onto the table and screamed, "I'll get you! When I get out of jail, I'll steal all your cats too!" Luckily the bailiff was able to drag the defendant off to the cells, unnecessarily banging his head on the door frame along the way (settling another important point — that the bailiff was definitely dreamier than the sandwich man).

The judge was very sorry the trial was over because he had been enjoying Nanny Piggins's cakes too. But she promised to bake him a special one all for himself, and to come down to the courthouse and yell "Guilty" at the defendants whenever she had the time. The judge tried to persuade Nanny Piggins to pursue a career in law, saying she had all the makings of an excellent Supreme Court justice. But Nanny Piggins politely refused. "I prefer the hours and workload of being a nanny. It allows more opportunity for lying on the couch eating baked goods."

"Very wise," said the judge.

And so Nanny Piggins, Boris, and the children returned home, satisfied that they had played their part in seeing that justice was served.

CHAPTER ELEVEN

The Westminster Nanny Show

anny Piggins was the first to admit that, while she had many, many, many great strengths, she also had one or two teensy-weensy weaknesses. For example, while she was a world leader at getting small children dirty, she was not quite so equally talented at getting them clean again.

I am sure Nanny Piggins could have been good at cleaning children if she wanted to, but she did not. In her opinion, there was little point getting children clean when they would only get dirty again. Plus, instinctively, she knew that the number of layers of dirt on the outside of the child was a good measure of the happiness of the child beneath.

That said, even Nanny Piggins realized that sometimes the Green children were so disgustingly filthy, she should be slightly ashamed. And on these rare occasions, Nanny Piggins always did the same thing—she sent the children on a playdate to visit their friends Samson and Margaret Wallace.

You see, the Wallace children had their own nanny, Nanny Anne. And she was the most fastidiously clean person, possibly on the planet (certainly in the top three). Nanny Piggins knew that if she sent Derrick, Samantha, and Michael over to the Wallace house, Nanny Anne would clean them. Not because she wanted them to be clean, but because Nanny Anne wanted to humiliate Nanny Piggins. Little did she realize that doing Nanny Piggins's job for her was not the way to embarrass Nanny Piggins.

"Please don't make us go and play there," begged Michael. "We'll clean ourselves."

"But you've got all that permanent marker on your arms where I was writing my shopping list on you. And there's all that oil-based paint in your hair from when I dared you to paint Mr. FitzPatrick's tree pink," argued Nanny Piggins. "Pen and paint are really difficult to get out."

"I don't mind if you shave my head," pleaded Michael.

"Look, I know it's horrible being forced to visit such an unnaturally clean house and eat health food and watch educational documentaries on television," said Nanny Piggins. "But I promise I will only leave you there for an hour. If you do desperately need rescuing before that, you can always ring and use the code word."

"What's the code word?" asked Derrick.

"Aaaaggghhh!" said Nanny Piggins.

"I think we can remember that," said Samantha.

"Now stand still while I wrap these sheets around you," said Nanny Piggins as she wrapped bedding around each of the children.

"Why are you wrapping sheets around us?" asked Derrick.

"I might as well get them cleaned too," said Nanny Piggins.

"Do you really think Nanny Anne will fall for that?" asked Samantha.

"If she doesn't clean them, she'll burn them. Either

way, it saves me from having to get the marmalade stains out," said Nanny Piggins. "If only there was some way we could send Boris on the playdate too. He's got a lot of honey matted into his fur."

"I definitely don't think Nanny Anne will fall for that," said Derrick. "Even she would rather not clean a ten-foot-tall dancing bear."

"You're right," agreed Nanny Piggins. "I'll just have to take him down to the fire station and get them to blast him with their hoses again."

So the Green children, wrapped in their bedsheets, trudged off to play with Samson and Margaret Wallace.

And Nanny Piggins was left alone in the house to enjoy a few rare quiet moments. So she got out a big block of chocolate and a big, thick romance novel and made herself comfortable on the couch. She had eaten half the block of chocolate and gotten up to a really good bit in the novel (where the heroine was just about to slap the hero really hard across the face) when the phone rang. Nanny Piggins's pig senses immediately told her something was wrong—it is a little-known fact that pigs have eight senses. As well as the regular five senses, pigs can also sense the threat of danger, the presence of chocolate, and the way to the nearest cinema. Nanny Piggins leaped for the phone, but all she heard was Derrick's scream of "Aaaa..." before the line went dead.

Fortunately Nanny Piggins was an elite athlete. So with all the speed and agility of a former flying pig, she leaped out the window (it was quicker than using the door), raced down the road to the Wallace house, and kicked the front door in with her trotter.

Nanny Anne was standing there with elbow-length rubber gloves, a scrubbing brush, and a two-gallon bottle of disinfectant, having backed Derrick, Samantha, and Michael into a corner.

"Nanny Piggins, how nice to see you," lied Nanny Anne.

"I've come to collect the children," said Nanny Piggins.

"But they've only been here twenty-five minutes," said Nanny Anne. "And we were hoping they would stay and play all afternoon."

"I've just remembered they've got a very important funeral to go to," lied Nanny Piggins.

"Children at a funeral?" said Nanny Anne. "That doesn't sound very likely."

"Their favorite great-uncle, Captain Balderdash, died, and they're giving the eulogy," embellished Nanny Piggins.

"All three of them?" asked Nanny Anne.

"Yes, they are going to take turns saying the words. It was a last request of Captain Balderdash. It will be a moving piece of performance art, encouraging the audience to think about man's inhumanity to man," said Nanny Piggins.

This was such an audacious lie that Nanny Anne was momentarily flummoxed, which gave Nanny Piggins the opportunity to run in; grab Derrick, Samantha, and Michael; and pull them out the door.

"Good-bye, Nanny Piggins," called Nanny Anne. "I expect I'll see you at the show on Monday."

Nanny Piggins was just slamming the front door when she heard this last sentence, so she stuck her trotter in the doorway (which hurt).

"What?" said Nanny Piggins. (She did not believe in saying "I beg your pardon" if you actually meant "What?")

"The Westminster Nanny Show starts on Monday," said Nanny Anne with a smile. "You are entered, aren't you? Such an accomplished nanny as yourself?"

Nanny Piggins was torn. She desperately wanted to slam the door in Nanny Anne's face and stomp off. But she also wanted to know what on earth Nanny Anne was talking about. So she took a deep breath, resisted the urge to hit Nanny Anne, and asked, "What is the Westminster Nanny Show?"

"You don't know?" asked Nanny Anne.

Nanny Piggins went red in the face. She looked like her head was going to explode from anger. The children knew these warning signs.

"Of course she doesn't know. That's why she asked," said Michael protectively.

"The Westminster Nanny Show is the premier international nannying competition," explained Nanny Anne. "Nannies from around the world travel here to compete. I was so sure with your 'unique' approach to child-raising, you would want to enter."

"Oh, I'm competing. In fact," lied Nanny Piggins, "I don't even have to enter. I was begged to compete by the organizers because the standard of nannying has been so poor in recent years. They wanted to bring in someone seriously good to show all the rest of you how it's done!"

"Really?" said Nanny Anne, which shows how annoyed she was, because she had run out of things to say that sounded polite but really were not.

"Yes, really," said Nanny Piggins. "So I guess I'll be beating you on Monday." And with that, Nanny Piggins turned and led the children away.

"I've cleaned your children for you," called Nanny Anne. "If Derrick gets that fungal rash behind his knees again, I used steel wool to scrub it off."

Nanny Piggins turned to run back and bite Nanny Anne. But the children grabbed their nanny in time before she could bite anything she would regret. (She had bitten Nanny Anne once when they first met, and Nanny Piggins had found the experience disgusting. Nanny Anne was so disinfected and clean that biting her was like having your mouth washed out with soap.)

"I really, really hope taekwondo is one of the things I can compete in at the Westminster Nanny Show," said Nanny Piggins as she visualized herself delivering a swift kick to Nanny Anne's solar plexus.

"I don't think it is," said Samantha sadly.

"Let's get a copy of the rules so we can go home and read them," said Nanny Piggins. "I want to thrash

Nanny Anne. And I want to do better than her in the Westminster Nanny Show as well."

Unfortunately, reading the rules did not make Nanny Piggins very happy.

"These rules are ridiculous!" exclaimed Nanny Piggins. "The competitions are for things like obedience and grooming. Who wants to be good at that? Why can't they have an event for blasting children from a cannon? I'd be sure to win then."

"Maybe they are worried that the other nannies wouldn't be as good at blasting children from a cannon as you and there might be horrible injuries," said Derrick.

"I suppose," conceded Nanny Piggins. "Gunpowder and artillery do bring out the worst in humans. But they could at least have ninja star throwing or leg biting. I could easily teach you children how to bite a leg in forty-eight hours."

"It might be too late to get the rules of the Westminster Nanny Show changed," said Samantha. "The rules have been the same for one hundred and fifty years. It would probably take more than two days to get all the judges together and persuade them to include ninja star throwing."

"I guess you're right," sighed Nanny Piggins. "So that means we have two days to learn obedience, grooming, and the obstacle course."

"Where should we start?" asked Michael.

"Well, that's obvious," said Nanny Piggins. "If we have all this work to do and we only have forty-eight hours to do it, then the very first thing we should do is go down to the bakery and eat some cake."

"Are you sure?" asked Samantha. "Eating cake doesn't sound very athletic."

"Oh yes, it is," Nanny Piggins assured her. "All marathon runners do it. Only they don't call it 'eating lots of cake'; they call it 'carbo-loading.'"

"If it's got a special name, then it must be all right," approved Michael.

So Nanny Piggins and the children headed out to the bakery for some carbo-loading. Unfortunately, things did not go quite as planned.

Sixteen long hours later, Nanny Piggins and the children returned to the house. They had not meant to be away that long. But at the bakery, Nanny Piggins got in an argument with Hans the baker about his chocolate tart, which ended up with her going back into his kitchen and showing him how a tart should be made. This led to a customer accidentally buying a slice of Nanny Piggins's tart. Which led to that customer insisting that Nanny Piggins and the children fly on his private jet with him to his country home so she could make the same tart for his wife. Which led to them staying for a seven-hour dinner party, with dancing and plate smashing (which was unusual because they were not even Greek).

Naturally, by the time Nanny Piggins and the children got home, they were tired and went to bed. When they woke up, there were only twenty hours left to prepare for the Westminster Nanny Show.

"So when do we start the training?" asked Samantha.

"Oh, it's too late to start training now," said Nanny Piggins as she sat down to eat her breakfast.

"What?!" exclaimed Derrick.

"We're all going to have to compete tomorrow," explained Nanny Piggins, "so it's very important that today we rest. It's called 'tapering down.' All marathon runners taper down."

"But we haven't done any training," protested Samantha. "We don't have anything to taper down from."

"Experience has taught me that it is always better to be well rested than to know what you're doing," said Nanny Piggins wisely.

"Are you sure?" said Michael. He enjoyed being lazy as much as the next boy, but he was not entirely convinced by Nanny Piggins's reasoning.

"Absolutely!" said Nanny Piggins. "The training regimen I have devised for today involves lying on the sofa with cucumbers over our eyes and watching TV."

"How can we have cucumbers over our eyes and watch TV?" asked Derrick.

"You're allowed to pick up the edge of the cucumber and peek when it gets to a good bit," explained Nanny Piggins.

And so that is exactly what they did.

As such, on Monday morning, Derrick, Samantha, and Michael awoke very well rested but completely unprepared for their day ahead. This did not seem to bother their nanny at all.

"Good morning, future champions," she said before whistling jauntily as she buttered her toast and ate just as many breakfast muffins as ever.

"Aren't you even the slightest bit nervous?" asked Samantha.

"When you've wrestled with Zulu warriors, given noogies to saltwater crocodiles, and played Pin the Tail on the Donkey with a real donkey, then it takes more than just a few simple games to make you nervous," said Nanny Piggins.

"I'd rather wrestle a crocodile than go head-to-head with Nanny Anne," said Derrick.

"Of course you would. That's only natural. Saltwater crocodiles are much nicer. But it is important to challenge yourself and confront your enemies," said Nanny Piggins.

"I thought you said it was best to run away from your enemies and eat cake," said Derrick, remembering something Nanny Piggins had made him commit to memory earlier.

"True," agreed Nanny Piggins. "I did say that. But it is a pig's prerogative to change her mind."

After breakfast Nanny Piggins and the children left for the Westminster Nanny Show. They took Boris with them, partly because he begged to come along, and partly because Nanny Piggins thought it would be handy to have him there in case any of the judges caused trouble and needed to be sat on.

Nanny Piggins was surprised when they arrived at the venue. She had expected the Westminster Nanny Show to be held in a church hall or the back room of a Rotary Club. She had not expected the enormous forty-thousand-seat arena they walked into. The stage area was lit up like a boxing ring. And the empty seats (soon to be filled by avid nannying fans) spread out into the darkness in every direction.

Nanny Piggins had assumed she would be competing against a dozen silly nannies like Nanny Anne. She had not expected to meet the group of fifty-nine competitors gathered from all around the world.

Nor had she imagined that they would all want to have their photograph taken with her.

"*Piggins san oai dekite koe desu!*" exclaimed the Japanese

nannies as they bowed repeatedly. (That is Japanese for "Miss Piggins, it is a great honor to meet you.")

"Why do all these nannies know you?" asked Derrick.

"I suppose it's because I write the occasional article for *Nannying Monthly*," explained Nanny Piggins. "I never realized that people actually read that magazine."

But they did. And once word spread that *the* Nanny Piggins had entered the building, even more international nannies were rushing forward and asking Nanny Piggins for her autograph.

"What do you say in these articles?" asked Samantha suspiciously.

"Well, mainly I tell them how stupid their magazine is and how all the articles in it are wrong," said Nanny Piggins.

"Are they?" said Derrick.

"Oh yes, they have these boring articles that go on for page after page about routines," explained Nanny Piggins.

"Routines?" asked Boris. "You mean, like, dance routines?"

"No, that would make some sense. But these articles are about daily routines," said Nanny Piggins. "They seem to think it is vitally important that children do exactly the same thing at exactly the same time every single day."

"What do they think happens if they don't?" asked Boris.

"The child grows up to be a serial killer," said Nanny Piggins. "Or worse, an actor."

"What a bizarre theory," puzzled Boris.

"Well, humans used to think the world was flat. They're not a terribly bright species," said Nanny Piggins.

"So what do you suggest in your articles?" asked Derrick.

"I emphasize the basics. Lots of fresh air. Which is why you must never allow children to attend school five days in a row, because there's no fresh air in a classroom," said Nanny Piggins. The children nodded. They had all heard this theory before. "And, of course, diet. Children must never go on one, because then they'll start talking about their diet. And nothing is more boring than someone talking about eating less."

Just then, a Swiss nanny came up to Nanny Piggins and shook her trotter. "Nanny Piggins, that article you wrote about letting children watch graphically violent movies in case they want to grow up to be ER doctors was the funniest thing I have ever read. Bravo!"

"Why did she say *funniest*?" asked Boris.

"It must be a translation problem," said Nanny Piggins. "I don't think people in Switzerland know what funny means. It's all that alpine air. Not enough oxygen gets to their brains."

But as the children looked about the room, they noticed that just seeing Nanny Piggins made the other nannies giggle as they remembered the things she had written in the articles.

"Nanny Piggins, I don't think these nannies take your articles seriously," said Samantha.

"What do you mean?" asked Nanny Piggins.

"Well, they keep looking at you, pointing, and laughing," explained Samantha.

"They are laughing at me?!" asked Nanny Piggins disbelievingly.

"The fools," muttered Boris, looking around for somewhere to hide. He knew that no one laughed at Nanny Piggins without suffering dire consequences.

"Well!" exclaimed Nanny Piggins. "I only came here to beat Nanny Anne and humiliate her in front of the entire world. But now, that's it. I'm going to stick it to the lot of them. These nannies will never laugh at me again!"

The first competition was grooming. Fifty-nine nannies lined up ready to go, with their charges in front of them, all immaculately groomed. The idea was to present the child absolutely scrubbed spotless and perfectly ironed (the backs of the ears were inspected with a microscope, so the washing had to be really thorough).

Nanny Piggins was entering Samantha in the grooming competition. Samantha did not fancy her chances. The other nannies had been cleaning their children for weeks in preparation, whereas Nanny Piggins only had ten minutes in a cleaner's storage room. But having been a flying pig for many years, Nanny Piggins knew how to get ready for a show, and a room full of solvents and industrial-strength cleaning equipment was the perfect place to do it. While the other nannies dabbed their children with talcum powder, Nanny Piggins attacked Samantha with a whirlwind of machinery and chemicals.

Boris, Derrick, and Michael were sitting with the crowd in the stands. All the seats in the stadium were now full, and there was an excited hum in the air as the nannies began to jog out into the arena with their children. Michael counted them as they came out. The first fifty-nine looked much the same. Neither the nannies nor the children had a hair out of place.

"Where's Nanny Piggins?" asked Derrick.

"I do hope she hasn't run off with one of the catering vans," worried Boris. "She does have lapses of judgment when she is around truckloads of food."

"Here she comes!" cried Michael excitedly, jumping up and down.

Nanny Piggins and Samantha had entered the arena. Whereas the other nannies had jogged sportily, Nanny Piggins and Samantha sashayed (Samantha did not look quite as comfortable doing this as Nanny Piggins, but she was putting in a good effort). And while all the other children were dressed in their school uniforms or Sunday-best clothes, Samantha was dressed in the latest designer clothes from Paris.

"Where did she get that dress?" asked Derrick.

"My sister is very good at sewing," explained Boris.

"She has a photographic memory for fashion. She only has to see an outfit once in a magazine and she can replicate it at a moment's notice. All she needs is some thread and a few old potato sacks."

"Samantha actually looks...good," said Michael (which is really the finest compliment, because admitting his sister looks good are the hardest words for any brother to say).

The judges, with their white coats and clipboards, stood huddled in a small group for some time. The crowd could tell they were arguing because there was a lot of animated hand waving and some chest prodding as well. But eventually they reached a decision, and a huge roar came from the crowd when it was announced that Nanny Piggins had won the grooming section. The judges did not really want to give it to her, but there was no denying that Samantha was clean. (She'd even passed the microscope-behind-the-ears test.) And it would have been very petty of them not to give bonus points for making a designer French outfit in under ten minutes. (Some judges did briefly consider being petty—but were actually quite glad not to have to give the win to Nanny Anne for the seventh year in a row.)

Nanny Anne was enraged. She had been sure that exposing Samson to dangerous amounts of ultraviolet light would clinch her the grooming section on hygiene points alone. Bacteria were afraid to go near him because he practically glowed.

The next stage of the competition was obedience. Now this was definitely the hardest part for Nanny Piggins because she barely knew what the word *obedience* meant. And when she found out, she thought it was utterly unimportant. If she ever caught Derrick, Samantha, and Michael doing exactly what she said, she would tell them off for not using their imaginations. So to be ordering Derrick around in a stadium was like torture to her—it was like eating hot toast without buttering it.

The other fifty-nine nannies went first. And to Nanny Piggins's eye, she could not see any difference in any of their performances. The only way the judges could separate them was by getting out rulers and protractors to see if the children's feet were perfectly aligned when they stood still. Or using a high-speed camera to see how many one-hundredths of a second it took the child to stop when their nanny said "stop."

Nanny Piggins had no interest in obedience. And

Derrick had no training in obedience. The only thing that gave them any chance against the other nannies was Derrick's love. Because Derrick loved his nanny a thousand times more than any of the other children loved their hygiene-obsessed careworkers. So when it came to their turn to stand in the center of the arena in front of forty thousand spectators, Derrick tried that much harder and cared that much more than any of the other children.

When Nanny Piggins said "stay" he stayed, when she said "fetch" he fetched, when she said "sit" he sat. He did everything just as well as Samson Wallace, much to the fury of Nanny Anne. Nanny Piggins was going to get an excellent mark for obedience because, even using protractors and high-speed cameras, the judges could not fault Derrick's obedience.

That was, until halfway through, when Nanny Piggins cracked.

"I can't take this anymore!" she screamed. Derrick looked worried. He knew what to do when Nanny Piggins said "sit," "fetch," or "stay." But he did not know what to do when she screamed "I can't take this anymore!"

"This is the stupidest thing I have ever heard of!!!" ranted Nanny Piggins. "Obedience?!! I mean, obedience?! What a ridiculous thing to—" Nanny Piggins was interrupted midyell by Boris barging his way out of the crowd, grabbing her, and dragging her off into the wings before she did something she regretted. So naturally Nanny Piggins did not get a very good mark for that part of the competition.

Having won the first event and come last in the second event, Nanny Piggins was ranked thirtieth overall. Nanny Anne was first. (If the final event had been a smirking competition, the trophy would have been hers already.) The final event was the obstacle course. The only way Nanny Piggins could beat Nanny Anne now was if Michael completed the obstacle course in half the time of any other child.

Now, you must remember that the other children had done actual training on this obstacle course, for months in fact. Whereas Michael had spent the previous months enjoying his favorite hobby, which was sitting under a bush in the garden eating un-defrosted frozen cake. Plus, the kindest way to describe Michael's physique would be to call him stout (and I dare not use any other word in case Nanny Piggins reads this book and comes to bite me). So lined up alongside all the other children, who were whippet-thin from being forced to get up and go jogging at four AM every day, Michael looked out of place.

Nanny Piggins was optimistic until she saw the other children in action. Even she had to admit they were seriously good. To complete the obstacle course, the children had to run through car tires, swing across a mud pit, crawl through a tunnel, and climb over a wall. And the way the other children performed, they could have been an act in the circus. They leaped, ran, and climbed with the agility of Chinese acrobats.

When Nanny Piggins's turn came around, she looked across at Michael. There were still smears of honey around his mouth from the snack he had been eating with Boris in the stands. At least he was not going to fail from lack of carbo-loading. For a split second a thought crossed Nanny Piggins's mind—that perhaps it was cruel to force this little boy to take part in such a potentially humiliating competition. Then Nanny Piggins had a brilliant idea.

Just as the judge raised the starting pistol in the air,

ready to fire, Nanny Piggins leaned in and whispered something in Michael's ear. Michael's eyes bugged wide, and as soon as he heard the gunshot, he took off.

The people who saw Michael in the stands that night saw something they will never forget. In decades to come, they will still be telling their grandchildren and great-grandchildren the story of the day they saw a boy move faster than the speed of light. Because Michael raced through that obstacle course like he had been bitten by a radioactive spider. He sprinted through the tires, swung over the mud pit, crawled through the tunnel, and leaped over the wall with grace and speed. He did not just do it in half the time of the other children, he did it in a third of the time.

The judges were so shocked by his brilliance, they immediately made him do a drug test and show them his birth certificate in case he was secretly a very short Olympic athlete pretending to be a chubby little boy.

But Michael passed the tests, and Nanny Piggins was awarded champion of the Westminster Nanny Show. Nanny Anne was seen fake-smiling so hard, she cracked a tooth. Nanny Piggins was so happy to win, she felt she could be magnanimous. So she only ran

The people who saw Michael in the
stands that night saw something
they will never forget.

around the ring three times, yelling, "Ha-hah! I beat you, I beat you all!"

The editor of *Nannying Monthly* rushed up, shook Nanny Piggins's trotter, and begged her to write a regular column for his magazine. "We've always known your articles were brilliantly funny. But we never realized you actually knew how to take care of children as well."

Of course Nanny Piggins said no, because writing abusive and insulting letters to magazines is fun as a hobby, but it takes all the joy out of it when it is a job.

So as Nanny Piggins, Boris, and the children hitched a lift home in one of the catering vans, they were all very happy. Nanny Piggins kept hugging the children each in turn, then all together, then Boris too, so he would not feel left out.

"What I don't understand is how on earth you were able to do the obstacle course so quickly," said Derrick.

"It was all the training I'd done," said Michael as he took a spoonful of the gallon of ice cream Nanny Piggins had bought him.

"But you didn't do any training," said Samantha.

"Yes, I did. We train all the time. How many times

have we had to leap over walls, crawl through hedges, and dodge around garden gnomes since Nanny Piggins has been our nanny?" asked Michael.

Derrick and Samantha thought about it, and they had to admit, the answer was quite a lot.

"And doing an obstacle course when there isn't a savage dog or a stick-wielding neighbor chasing you is actually much easier," explained Michael.

"But Nanny Piggins said something to you just before the starter's pistol. Something that made you run extra fast, didn't she?" asked Boris.

Michael smiled. "Yes, she did."

"What was it?" asked Derrick and Samantha.

"She said—" said Michael.

Boris, Derrick, and Samantha leaned in close to hear the secret. "She said she would buy me a gallon of ice cream if we won."

"Could there be any greater motivation?" declared Nanny Piggins before giving them each, then all together, another hug.

CHAPTER TWELVE

Nanny Piggins and the Gypsy Wedding

Nanny Piggins was teaching the children to pick a lock. Partly because she thought it was an important life skill, but mainly because she had forgotten her keys and locked herself out of the house. This would not have mattered so much if they had not just bought ten gallons of chocolate chip ice cream, which urgently needed to go in the freezer. Consequently, Nanny Piggins was desperately racing Boris to see whether she could break into the house quicker than he could eat the ice cream.

Boris seemed to be winning. Nanny Piggins was very good at picking locks with a hairpin. But the problem is, if you have a hairpin, then you have the type of hair that needs to be pinned up. Which means, if you take the pin out, your hair will fall in your face and distract you. Plus Nanny Piggins could not stand having unattractive hair, even when she was breaking and entering into her own home in an urgent attempt to rescue ice cream.

Her lock-picking lesson, however, soon became irrelevant when a man barged past her, screaming, "Get out of the way!!!"

The man slammed into the locked door, which only momentarily stopped him because he was hefty enough and moving with enough speed to break the lock and the door frame, smashing the door open and landing sprawled on the inside doormat.

When Nanny Piggins stepped into the hallway and turned on the light, she was shocked to discover that the screaming man was, in fact, Mr. Green himself.

"It's your father!" gasped Nanny Piggins.

"Do you think he's gone insane?" asked Michael optimistically.

"Years ago," said Nanny Piggins. "But he seems extra especially bad right now."

"Close the door! Quickly close the door!" begged Mr. Green.

Boris pushed the door closed. (Mr. Green did not even ask why there was a ten-foot-tall dancing bear in his home, which shows just how distracted he was.)

"Now lock it!" pleaded Mr. Green.

"We can't lock it," said Derrick. "You just smashed the lock."

"Then fetch me a hammer and nails," ordered Mr. Green.

Michael ran as quickly as he could to the shed and back with the required equipment. His father rarely used tools, so he knew this was going to be entertaining. And it was. As soon as Mr. Green began nailing the door shut, it became clear he had no idea what he was doing. He kept banging himself on the hand or dropping the hammer on his foot.

After she had finished laughing (and finished eating

the remaining six gallons of ice cream), Nanny Piggins took pity on Mr. Green. She took the hammer and sealed the door with a few vicious but well-aimed wallops.

"Now, Mr. Green, why don't you come into the living room and tell us what is going on?" suggested Nanny Piggins.

"No time," muttered Mr. Green manically. "I must pack my bags. Consult my lawyer. Book an airplane ticket to a secret foreign location."

"Why? Have you killed someone?" asked Samantha.

"No, no," said Mr. Green.

"Does someone want to kill you?" asked Nanny Piggins. She knew at least two dozen people off the top of her head who definitely did. "Apart from the usual people, I mean."

"It's worse than that," said Mr. Green.

"Someone wants to force you to study calculus?" suggested Derrick.

"No, much, much worse. There's a woman—" said Mr. Green.

"No way!" interrupted Nanny Piggins.

"And she wants to marry me!" said Mr. Green.

At this point Nanny Piggins lost track of what Mr. Green was saying because she had fainted. Now you have to remember, Nanny Piggins had seen rebellions, earthquakes, and circus clowns without their makeup, all without ever batting an eye. So for Nanny Piggins to be so totally shocked that her body stopped pumping blood to her head really says something.

Boris wafted chocolate cake under Nanny Piggins's nose to revive her. They knew she was coming around when her eyelids began to flutter and she snapped the slice out of Boris's hand, nearly amputating one of his fingers.

"I'm sorry, children," apologized Nanny Piggins. "I must have had a dream. I thought I heard your father say that a woman wanted to marry him."

"He did," said Derrick.

"Quick, more cake," called Samantha as Nanny Piggins's eyes rolled back in her head and she started to faint again.

Half a chocolate mud cake later, Nanny Piggins had revived enough to hear the rest of Mr. Green's story.

"I went to one of those speed-dating evenings," began Mr. Green.

"An evening where you quickly eat dates?" queried Boris.

"No, it's an evening where you go on lots of two-minutes dates with lots of different women because you are scared they will find out what you are really like if they talk to you for longer," explained Derrick.

"So it's got nothing to do with sticky date pudding?" asked Boris.

"No," admitted Derrick.

"What a shame," sighed Boris. He was particularly fond of sticky date pudding.

"So what happened?" asked Nanny Piggins.

"I met a woman..." began Mr. Green.

"I wish I hadn't eaten all that chocolate cake. I'm starting to feel sick listening to this," said Nanny Piggins.

"And she fell in love with me," said Mr. Green.

"Was this speed-dating held in a very dark room?" asked Nanny Piggins.

"No," said Mr. Green pathetically.

"Are you sure it wasn't just an elaborate practical joke?" asked Nanny Piggins. "Perhaps one of your colleagues wanted to get back at you for being an insufferable bore."

"I don't think so," said Mr. Green. "When they want to do that, they usually just steal my yogurt from the lunchroom fridge."

"I wouldn't worry," Nanny Piggins assured him. "I'm sure when this woman wakes up tomorrow morning, her friends will hold some sort of intervention for her. She will realize she has made a terrible mistake and never want to see you again."

"But it's been a week already! I went speed-dating last Friday, and she has been stalking me ever since," sobbed Mr. Green. "She turns up at the office, bumps into me in the street, and showers me with gifts."

"What sort of gifts?" asked Nanny Piggins.

"Chocolates," whimpered Mr. Green.

"Then what's the problem?" asked Nanny Piggins, totally perplexed.

"This morning, she cornered me in the elevator," blubbered Mr. Green, "and...and...she proposed to me!" With that, Mr. Green totally broke down.

"But I thought you wanted to get married?" said Derrick.

"I do. But I want to marry a nice, quiet woman," sobbed Mr. Green.

"Who is easy to ignore?" suggested Nanny Piggins.

"Exactly," said Mr. Green.

"And this woman is not easy to ignore?" guessed Nanny Piggins.

"She is impossible to ignore," declared Mr. Green.

"You'll be fine," Nanny Piggins assured him. "You're safe here because she doesn't know where you live."

(Now, dear reader, having read the first eleven chapters of this book, you will have realized that Nanny Piggins is rarely wrong. But this is one occasion where she has made a boo-boo. In fact, she was not just wrong, she was really, really wrong. For not only did the woman Mr. Green had met at speed-dating know where he lived, she was actually, at that very moment, hiding in a bush in the front yard watching the Green house. She had been there the whole time. She had seen Mr. Green barge his way in. She had heard Nanny Piggins nail the door shut. And she had watched through the window as they sent Mr. Green to bed and then stayed up eating the other half of the mud cake and giggling about Mr. Green's predicament. So having watched the house so closely, Arianna Rommanickle knew exactly when everyone inside had gone to bed and gone to sleep.)

The next morning, Nanny Piggins and the children were halfway through breakfast before they noticed something peculiar.

"There is something odd about this morning," said Nanny Piggins, sniffing the air.

"What is it?" asked Derrick.

"I'm not sure. But for some reason this breakfast food tastes even better than normal," said Nanny Piggins.

"Perhaps there's extra sugar in the marmalade," said Michael.

"I know there's extra sugar in the marmalade because I put twelve teaspoons in myself," said Nanny Piggins. "But there's something else. The sun seems to be shining brighter, the birds seem to be singing more sweetly, the world seems to be a happier place this morning."

They all looked around the room trying to figure out what it was. It was several moments before Samantha exclaimed, "I know what it is! Father's not here!"

They all turned to look at Mr. Green. And Samantha was quite right. He was not there. His seat was empty.

"What a lovely surprise!" said Nanny Piggins delightedly.

And they all went back to eating their breakfast.

But after a few moments more, a thought occurred to Derrick. "Why isn't he here?"

This question stumped Nanny Piggins. Mr. Green certainly would not skip breakfast just so they could enjoy their meal.

"Perhaps he's sleeping in," suggested Nanny Piggins.

"He doesn't like to sleep," said Michael. "He can't bill the time to a client."

"Perhaps he's gone to work without breakfast," guessed Nanny Piggins.

"He doesn't like to get breakfast at work," said Samantha, "because then he has to pay for it."

"I suppose we should check his room," said Nanny Piggins reluctantly.

The children agreed to this idea. But they also agreed to finish their breakfast first. If something dreadful had happened to their father, it would be better to celebrate on a full stomach.

A short time later, Nanny Piggins and the children stood outside Mr. Green's bedroom door, unsure what to do. They wanted to find out what had happened to him. But they did not want to burst in and see him wearing anything less than a three-piece suit.

"Mr. Green, are you in there?" called Nanny Piggins tentatively.

There was no reply.

"Why don't we just wait a week or two?" suggested Nanny Piggins. "If he is in there, we'll find out eventually. And if he's not, does it matter whether we know?"

"I need him to sign my permission slip to go to the zoo," said Michael. "And the zoo won't accept your signature ever since the time you let the giraffe out to stretch his legs."

"Oh dear," said Nanny Piggins. "Then there is nothing for it. We shall have to go in. Cover your eyes, children, in case there is anything shocking in there."

Nanny Piggins covered her own eyes, then kicked the door in with her trotter. (The door was actually unlocked, but she enjoyed kicking in a door. It added a certain drama to any tense situation.) Then, summoning the courage to peek through her trotters, Nanny Piggins discovered there was nothing shocking in Mr. Green's bedroom at all. Not even Mr. Green was in Mr. Green's bedroom. His bed was empty. The window was open. And the curtains were flapping in the breeze.

"Father's gone!" exclaimed Michael.

"Hooray!!!" screamed Derrick, Samantha, Michael, and Nanny Piggins simultaneously.

When they had finished dancing and hugging each other with excitement, they looked around the room. What they would have noticed immediately, if their eyes had not been clouded by tears of joy, was the note stabbed into the wall with a ruby-studded dagger directly above Mr. Green's bed.

"That's a nice dagger," said Nanny Piggins conversationally. "Rubies always remind me of strawberry jam."

"Perhaps we should read the note," suggested Samantha.

Nanny Piggins, Derrick, and Michael groaned.

"I don't want to either," protested Samantha, "but when your father goes missing and someone stabs a message into the wall with a dagger, you could get in trouble with the police if you don't even read the note."

"I suppose so," moaned Nanny Piggins as she removed the knife from the wall and took a closer look at the slip of paper. The note had been written in purple ink, and it read:

I have taken Mr. Green to be my new husband. Do not bother to come looking for him. I shan't let you have him back. Yours sincerely,

> *HRH Arianna Rommanickle*
> *Queen of the Gypsies*

"He's been kidnapped by the Queen of the Gypsies," marveled Derrick.

"Cool!" exclaimed Michael.

"I guess that means we can stay up late and watch horror movies tonight, then," said Nanny Piggins.

"Come along, children. You don't want to be late for school."

"But shouldn't we rescue Father?" asked Samantha.

Nanny Piggins, Derrick, and Michael thought about this for several moments.

"We could," said Nanny Piggins. "But I don't see that we have to. He wanted a wife and now he's got one. We shouldn't interfere."

"But we need Father to pay for our food," said Samantha, knowing this argument would weigh strongly with her nanny.

Nanny Piggins turned pale. "Leaping lamingtons!! You're right!" she exclaimed. "Quick, children! We must rescue your father immediately."

It took three minutes for Nanny Piggins to gather all the essential equipment (compass, rope, grappling hook, and chocolate) as well as the children and Boris into Mr. Green's car.

"Let's go!" declared Nanny Piggins.

"But where are we going?" asked Samantha. "How are we going to find them?"

"That's easy," said Nanny Piggins. "Gypsies wander randomly wherever their fancy takes them. So all we have to do is wander randomly and we should soon stumble across them."

"Are you entirely sure that will work?" asked Derrick skeptically.

"Do you have a better idea?" asked Nanny Piggins.

None of them did. So they set out, with Nanny Piggins behind the wheel,[8] driving in whichever direction she liked. Amazingly, whether through bizarre coincidence or because Nanny Piggins and the Queen of the Gypsies thought in much the same way, Nanny Piggins's plan worked perfectly. They stumbled across Arianna Rommanickle's campsite in just seven short hours.

Nanny Piggins, Boris, and the children sat in Mr. Green's vomit-yellow Rolls-Royce and watched the gypsy campsite. There were a dozen old caravans arranged in a circle. They knew which caravan belonged to the Gypsy Queen because it had the largest television antennas on the roof, the biggest flower

---

[8] Rest assured, by this stage Nanny Piggins had obtained a driver's license. Fortunately the driving examiner had fallen in love with her at first sight (and her chocolate brownies at first taste), so he was willing to overlook her total disregard for the road rules and the fact that the only way her trotters could reach the pedals was by driving standing up.

boxes on the windows, and the words ARIANNA ROMMANICKLE: GYPSY QUEEN written on the side.

"How are we going to do this?" asked Boris. "Do you want me to do a ballet dance to distract them?"

"No, a performance by a ballet dancer of your caliber would be too much of a reward. They have been very naughty and they don't deserve a treat," said Nanny Piggins.

"You don't think she's hurt Father, do you?" asked Samantha.

"Probably not. We could wait until she does if you like," said Nanny Piggins.

"Better not," said Derrick. "I'd like to be home in time to see the late movie on TV."

"So what is your plan?" asked Boris.

"I thought we could go up to the front door of Queen Arianna's caravan and ask nicely if she would return him," admitted Nanny Piggins.

"Do you think she would fall for that?" asked Michael.

"She might," said Nanny Piggins. "If she is crazy enough to want to marry your father, who knows what might fool her?"

And so Nanny Piggins, Boris, and the children made

their way through the campsite to the Gypsy Queen's caravan. The other gypsies in the camp left what they were doing and followed them, ready to watch. They had never seen a pig, a bear, and three children confront their queen before.

Nanny Piggins reached up and knocked boldly on the caravan's door.

"Yes?" called Queen Arianna from the other side of the closed door.

"Hello, Your Majesty. My name is Nanny Piggins and I've come to rescue Mr. Green," called Nanny Piggins.

The letter flap in the door opened and a heavily made-up eyeball appeared. The eyeball looked Nanny Piggins up and down.

"Very well," said Queen Arianna. "Come in."

Nanny Piggins, Boris, and the children entered the caravan. While it looked plain and ordinary on the outside, the inside was the exact opposite. It was amazing. There was a living room, kitchen, bathroom, and boudoir all mushed into one tiny room. And every surface, appliance, and ornament was covered in bright red, pink, or purple lace. It made Nanny Piggins's eyes hurt to look around.

Although, by far the most amazing thing in the room was Queen Arianna Rommanickle herself. Nanny Piggins had assumed that anybody who wanted to marry Mr. Green would be his female equivalent: slightly overweight, boring, and unsmiling. But this was not Queen Arianna at all. She was spectacular.

She was not much taller than Nanny Piggins, at four-foot-ten. But she had raven-black hair, deep dark eyes, and long hypnotic eyelashes like a Jersey cow. And most spectacularly, she was dressed in a huge fluffy white wedding dress. Nanny Piggins had never seen a woman with such style and panache (except when she looked in the mirror).

Meanwhile, a very sorry specimen sat in the corner. His conservative pajamas had been taken from him and replaced with bright green trousers, a red shirt, and a purple neckerchief.

"Who is that?" whispered Samantha.

"It's your father," whispered Nanny Piggins. "He's dressed like a gypsy."

Samantha had to stuff the sleeve of her sweater in her mouth to stop herself from laughing.

"We're terribly sorry to disturb you, Your Queenship," said Nanny Piggins. (It is always wise to be polite when talking with royalty.) "But could we please have Mr. Green back?"

"No," declared Queen Arianna. "I cannot let you have him back. I have decided he will be my new husband."

"But why?" asked Nanny Piggins. "You're so beautiful, you could do much better."

"I know. But I have always been attracted to weak, cowardly men. So I find your Mr. Green powerfully alluring," announced Arianna, as she affectionately played with his overgreased hair.

"I think I'm going to gag," said Derrick.

"The only thing is," said Nanny Piggins diplomatically, "he is father to these three children, and they need him to come home."

"It is too late. I am in love with Mr. Green. And the heart wants what it wants," declared Queen Arianna defiantly. "In a few hours he shall be my king and I shall be Queen Green."

"Hmm," said Nanny Piggins. "But from my understanding of ancient gypsy law, a betrothal can be challenged." (Nanny Piggins knew quite a lot about ancient gypsy law, having once been in a property dispute with a gypsy over a particularly delicious candy apple.)

"Yes," conceded Arianna. "But there is only one way you can make that challenge."

"I know," said Nanny Piggins. "Hand-to-hand combat."

The children and Boris gasped.

"Father has to fight her?" asked Derrick. Arianna might be half Mr. Green's height and a third his weight, but there was no doubt in Derrick's mind that she could destroy him easily.

"No, either a woman or a pig must battle for the man. And as I am both, I shall fight," declared Nanny Piggins.

"Very well," declared Arianna. "We shall fight for Mr. Green with sticks"—she paused dramatically— "over the pit of fire!"

"Couldn't you just play Monopoly?" asked Michael, suddenly afraid of what they had gotten their beloved nanny into.

"It's all right. It will take more than a stick and a pit

of fire to frighten me," said Nanny Piggins. "After all, I am a Piggins."

And so the preparations began. They actually took quite a long while because it takes a lot of time to dig a pit, build a fire, and get out of a wedding dress. (For some reason wedding-dress-makers have never heard of zippers.)

"Are you sure you want to go through with this, Nanny Piggins?" asked Samantha. "We could probably get along quite well without Father. Derrick and I could lie about our ages and go out and get jobs."

"I wouldn't dream of it!" declared Nanny Piggins. "It is bad enough that I have to have a job. I wouldn't think of inflicting employment on you."

"But is Father worth it?" asked Derrick.

"Not really," admitted Nanny Piggins. "But it is the principle of the matter. If we let one strange woman kidnap your father, then they'll all want to do it. We have to draw the line somewhere."

"But you will be careful, won't you?" sobbed Boris. "What would I do without my beloved sister?"

"You would look after the children and become their nanny," said Nanny Piggins firmly. "They will need someone to scare away the truancy officer when they take a day off school."

"I'll try," sniffled Boris.

"Oh, and Boris," said Nanny Piggins, "there's no need to cry. Think of Peru."

And so Nanny Piggins, Boris, and the children followed Queen Arianna to the pit of fire. The sun had gone down and the glowing red coals looked very scary. The children started to sweat from the heat throbbing off the flames. All the gypsies from the camp had gathered around the edge to watch. There was a log lying across the pit, just above the coals, and Queen Arianna faced Nanny Piggins, ready to step onto the log from the opposite side.

"Oh dear, oh dear, oh dear," sobbed Boris.

"I don't like this," said Michael, holding Samantha's hand.

Samantha did not say anything. She was worrying too much to think of words. She just bit her lip really hard. And Derrick pinched his leg to try to distract his tear ducts from crying.

"Let's get on with it," said Nanny Piggins briskly. "I want to get home in time for dinner."

"The winner of this contest gets to keep Mr. Green," announced Queen Arianna formally.

"Which means the loser wins too," said Nanny Piggins brightly as she picked up a long, heavy stick and stepped onto the log. Arianna stepped on at the other end. Nanny Piggins could feel the blaze from the coals sizzling at her legs.

Nanny Piggins was not a pig who was big on reflection. She found that thinking about things before you did them only ever muddled you up. If she was going to beat the Queen of the Gypsies senseless and push her into a pit of fire, better to get on with it. So Nanny Piggins raised her stick high and ran at Arianna, screaming, "Hiiiiyaaaaaaahhhhh!"

Now Queen Arianna was very good at fighting. Mr. Green was not the first husband she had taken without asking. So stick-fighting over a fire pit was something she was very familiar with. She was not, however, familiar with Nanny Piggins. Arianna did not realize quite what she had taken on until she was lying flat on her back being hit on the head with a stick for the seventh time.

Queen Arianna tried to hit Nanny Piggins back, but

she could not, because her own stick had fallen into the coals and had just burst into flames. It was at this moment that Queen Arianna began to suspect that she had made a dreadful mistake suggesting a fight to the death over a pit of fire. These things always seem like a good idea if you are going to win, but a bad idea when you are about to lose.

Fortunately for the Gypsy Queen, however, Nanny Piggins did a surprising thing. She did not push Queen Arianna off the log. Instead Nanny Piggins somersaulted over her, landing catlike on the far side of the pit, and ran off into the darkness of the night.

Arianna was stunned for one-eighth of a second. Then her brain started to work. Where were the children and the bear? She looked up and they were gone. And the pig had run off into the night. That could only mean one thing...

"She's tricked me! She's stolen my husband!" screamed Queen Arianna. All the gypsies began rushing in every direction, pretending to do something so they would not get in trouble. But it was too late. By the time they had found flashlights and started searching the bushes for the runaways, Nanny Piggins had

Queen Arianna began to suspect that she had made a dreadful mistake suggesting a fight to the death over a pit of fire.

already made it to the main road. And she only had to wait a few moments before Boris pulled up in Mr. Green's car with the children in the backseat.

"You didn't die!" exclaimed Boris as he sobbed into his sister's shoulder.

"Well done, Boris," said Nanny Piggins. "Just like in Peru, when you went and got the car while I distracted the Peruvian bandits by hitting them all repeatedly on the head."

"Oh, Nanny Piggins, what a relief!" exclaimed Samantha as she and her brothers hugged Nanny Piggins as hard as they could.

"Come along," said Nanny Piggins after making sure she had hugged them all three times each. "We need to get you home. You've had a difficult day, and you haven't had a thing to eat since those ten gallons of ice cream this morning."

And so Nanny Piggins, Boris, and the Green children enjoyed their ride home because they were safe and together just as a family should be.

It was only when they had been driving for about an hour that a thought occurred to Nanny Piggins.

"Where is your father? You did rescue him, didn't you? While I distracted all the gypsies?"

"Of course we rescued him," said Boris. "What sort of people do you think we are?"

"Then where is he?" asked Nanny Piggins, looking around the car that Mr. Green clearly was not in.

"We put him in the trunk," admitted Derrick.

"He wouldn't stop complaining," said Michael.

"We can stop and let him in the car if you like," said Samantha.

"It would be silly to stop now, when we are only six hours from home," said Nanny Piggins.

And so Nanny Piggins, Boris, and the children enjoyed a lovely car ride home. It actually took them eight hours because they had to stop several times. First for pizza, then for chocolate cake, and then for sticky date pudding (Boris had had it on his mind all day). And the eight hours in the trunk did Mr. Green no harm at all. He used the time to vow to himself over and over that he would never try to remarry again.

The world's most glamorous high-flying pig
is back with more sidesplitting
adventures in

NANNY PIGGINS
AND THE RUNAWAY LION
Available spring 2014!

Turn the page for a peek at the next installment
in the Nanny Piggins series!

CHAPTER ONE

Nanny Piggins and the Foreign Exchange Student

an anyone remember what the figurines looked like?" asked Nanny Piggins.

"All I can remember is that they were ugly," said Boris.

Nanny Piggins, Boris, and the children were in the living room looking at the shattered remnants of the late Grandma Green's figurine collection. The ten miniature statues had accidentally been smashed in a particularly athletic game of charades. (Nanny Piggins had set a vase of flowers on fire when acting out the book title *Bonfire of the Vanities*.

Then she had to leap to safety before her hair was caught in the inferno.)

"I think one of the figurines was a woman with a dog," said Michael. As a seven-year-old boy, he naturally had an affinity with dogs.

"I'm pretty sure those green bits were a mermaid," said Derrick, who, as an eleven-year-old, was developing an eye for mermaids.

"And one was a milkmaid with a cow...or a goat... but definitely something you milked," added Samantha. Being a nine-year-old who worried a lot, she did not like to commit to a decision.

"I know what we can do," said Nanny Piggins. "Let's recombine all the pieces to make one giant figurine of a monkey!"

"Why a monkey?" asked Boris.

"Everyone likes monkeys," said Nanny Piggins.

The others nodded at the truth of this statement.

"Which just goes to show," continued Nanny Piggins, "you can scratch yourself, slap your head, and bite tourists, but if you do it with enough charm, people will still think you're adorable."

So they set to work. Nanny Piggins was extremely

good with superglue. When you smashed as many Ming vases as she had in her time you needed to be. They had just reached the point where all ten of their hands were required to hold everything in place while the glue set when Mr. Green walked into the room.

"Wah!" said Boris as he ducked under the table. Then "Ow!" as he realized he had just ripped out a chunk of fur because he had accidentally superglued his paw to the figurine. Fortunately Mr. Green did not notice the ten-foot-tall dancing bear hiding under the table, because he was a very unobservant man. And the brain tends not to process information that is impossible to believe.

"Hello, children," said Mr. Green.

They all immediately knew something terrible was wrong because Mr. Green usually never spoke to the children except to tell them to "Go away" or "Be quiet" or "Stop pestering me for lunch money." Also, he was smiling, a skill he was very bad at. Mr. Green's smiles were frightening. Like a baboon baring his teeth right before he poops on his hand and throws it at you.

"Hello," said Nanny Piggins conversationally. "We were just polishing your beloved figurine. What do you think?"

Mr. Green leaned forward and peered at it. They all held their breaths as they waited to see if he would notice the difference between the ten original figurines and the giant one they were now holding.

"It looks fine," said Mr. Green.

They sighed with relief.

"But…" he continued.

They held their breaths again.

"Has it always been furry?" Mr. Green asked, looking at the brown tuft now stuck to the monkey's neck.

"Oh yes," said Nanny Piggins. "Embedded bear fur is the signature mark of a genuine antique Staffordshire flatback."

"Really? Well, my mother had quite the eye," said Mr. Green proudly. (It is funny how people grow fond of the relatives who once terrified them after they are safely dead.)

"Don't let us keep you from your tax law work," hinted Nanny Piggins as she politely tried to get rid of Mr. Green. "I know you must have something dreadfully important to do in your office. Paper clips to straighten and rebend, or some such."

This comment slightly unnerved Mr. Green because that was exactly what he had spent four hours doing only that morning, and then billed the time to a rich, old widow who was too nearsighted to check her invoice.

"Oh no, I came in here to make an announcement," he said. "You children are very lucky."

The children groaned. They knew something terrible was coming if their father thought they were lucky.

"What have you done?" Nanny Piggins glowered, suspecting him of trying to sell them for medical experiments again. "The hospital told you clearly. They don't accept donated organs from living people."

"No, this is another idea, even better. I've arranged a wonderful educational opportunity for the three of you," continued Mr. Green. He really was beginning to look very smug.

"What sort of wonderful educational opportunity?" asked Nanny Piggins, bracing herself to launch, teeth first, at his leg.

"Well, you see, a fellow at work was telling me about his son and how he sent him away as an exchange student," said Mr. Green.

"And how does that affect Derrick, Samantha, and Michael?" asked Nanny Piggins suspiciously.

"I thought it sounded like such a good idea I've enrolled them in an exchange-student program!" said Mr. Green triumphantly, whipping the paperwork out of his pocket and waving it in their faces. "It's all arranged. By the end of next week, they'll be off to Nicaragua for six months." Mr. Green was positively glowing with happiness. The idea of six months without his own children pleased him immensely.

"But I don't want to go to Nicaragua!" protested Nanny Piggins. "I've been there twice already, and while the turtles are nice and *gallo pinto* is delicious, the humid weather makes it very difficult to do anything with my hair."

"*You* won't be going," said Mr. Green.

"But what will Nanny Piggins do while we're away?" worried Samantha.

"Find a new job, of course," said Mr. Green.

"Noooooo!" yelled Michael. Being the youngest, he was more prone to outbursts of emotion. He would have flung himself at his father in a rage, but, like Boris, he had accidentally glued his hands to the figurine.

And Derrick tried to kick his father's shin under the table. Unfortunately, as he was only eleven years old, his legs weren't long enough to reach.

"I'm sure Miss Piggins will find work somewhere else," said Mr. Green. "Perhaps"—he started to laugh here as though he had thought of something funny—"perhaps she can get a job"—again he actually chortled—"in a bacon factory."

The children gasped and Boris banged his head on the dining table as he flinched away in horror. There was no greater insult to a pig than to mention the word *bacon*. Mr. Green's idea of a joke had mortally offended Nanny Piggins. If it were not for the fact that she, like Michael and Boris, had too much superglue on her trotters and was now stuck to the figurine, Mr. Green would have been in terrible trouble. As it was, she dragged the giant figurine three feet across the table as she lunged toward him.

Mr. Green cowered away. "It is all legitimate. Lots of parents do it. It's educational," he protested, the way people always protest when they have done something very bad and are about to be punished for it.

"I suggest you leave the room now, Mr. Green," said

Nanny Piggins, "to allow the children and me time to control our emotions."

Emotions of all varieties scared Mr. Green, so he did as he was told. He scuttled away and drove back to the office.

"What are we going to do?" wailed Samantha. She was not normally given to wailing, but the prospect of six months in Nicaragua can have that effect on a girl.

"Obviously we will have to thwart your father," said Nanny Piggins. "It really is exhausting putting him in his place all the time. I wonder if we got him a futon whether we could persuade him to sleep in his office and never come home."

"Do you have a plan?" asked Michael hopefully. He would actually have quite liked to go to Nicaragua because he was an adventurous boy and was, of course, intrigued by turtles. But he did not want to be separated from Nanny Piggins. She was the only family the children had. If you did not count their father. And none of them did.

"I have the beginning of an idea," admitted Nanny Piggins as she thoughtfully rubbed her snout. (She had to rub it on her arm because, of course, her trotters were glued to the figurine.)

"What do we have to do?" asked Derrick, desperate to take some sort of action.

"Well, for a start, we have to resmash this figurine," said Nanny Piggins.

"To teach Father a lesson?" asked Samantha.

"That is an added benefit. But the main reason is because we're all stuck to it. And I've run out of nail polish remover, so I've got nothing to dissolve the glue," said Nanny Piggins.

So after smashing the figurine back into a thousand pieces, and leaving it there because Mr. Green did not deserve to have it refixed, the children went off to school. Nanny Piggins assured them that she would soon solve the problem. Two weeks was a lot of time. She was sure to think of something.

The family was sitting around the breakfast table the next morning, which was not a pleasant experience for Mr. Green. He kept getting hit in the head with slices of toast. Michael claimed they were slipping out of his hands when he buttered them, but Mr. Green suspected that his youngest son might have been throwing them intentionally. Suddenly, there was a knock at the front door.

"Who could that be?" demanded Mr. Green.

"I expect it is someone at the front door," explained Nanny Piggins slowly and clearly. "They probably want you to open the door and speak to them."

"One of you children go," said Mr. Green dismissively.

"The children shouldn't answer the door to strangers," chided Nanny Piggins.

"Then you answer it," said Mr. Green.

"Very well," said Nanny Piggins, primping her hair as she got up from the table. "But if it is someone important who has come to give you a medal for services to tax law, are you sure you want the door to be answered by a pig, even if she is the most glamorous pig in the entire world?"

"All right, I'll do it myself," grumbled Mr. Green. As far as he was concerned, the fewer people who knew he housed a pig the better. Little did he realize, however, that while a great number of people knew

Nanny Piggins lived in the house, almost no one knew (or cared) whether Mr. Green even existed.

Nanny Piggins and the children followed him, curious to see who would pay Mr. Green a visit at breakfast time.

Mr. Green flung open the front door. "What do you want?" he demanded rudely. Then he immediately had to look down because the person he was being rude to was two feet shorter than he was expecting.

"*Bonjour, Monsieur* Green," said the diminutive boy standing on the doorstep. "My name is François. I am eleven years old and from Belgium. And I am to be your exchange student. It is a great pleasure to be welcomed to your country!" François then reached up, grabbed Mr. Green's head, pulled him down, and kissed him once on each cheek.

Mr. Green practically went into shock as François picked up his little suitcase and entered the house.

"*Bonjour*, I am François," François said to Nanny Piggins and the Green children.

"*Bonjour*," said Derrick, Samantha, and Michael.

"Thank you for welcoming me into your home," continued François with impeccable politeness and a lovely little bow. "I look forward to immersing myself in your culture."

"What does 'immerse yourself in culture' mean?" Michael whispered to Derrick.

"I think he wants to dip himself in yogurt," Derrick guessed.

"Now just you wait here," spluttered Mr. Green. "What is the meaning of this? Coming into my house with a suitcase and speaking French. It just isn't acceptable."

"But you are Mr. Green, yes?" asked François, looking just the right amount of confused and hurt to make even Mr. Green feel slightly guilty for raising his voice.

"Well, yes," admitted Mr. Green, secretly wishing he was not.

"And you signed up to join the Friends Around the World exchange-student program, did you not?" François asked.

"He did indeed," said Nanny Piggins. "We all saw the paperwork yesterday."

"Yes, but that was to send my children *away*," protested Mr. Green.

"Of course," said François. "But before your children go, you must first host a student in your home. That is the way the system works. Didn't you read the fine print of the contract?"

Mr. Green had not. Which was unusual because he was a lawyer and it was his job to write fine print into contracts. So he should have known better than anyone how devious fine print can be. But when he was at the exchange-student office, he had been so euphoric at the idea of six months without his children he had been too giddy for reading. Instead he had been busily fantasizing about closing up the children's bedrooms and saving money by disconnecting the electricity to all but one room in the house.

"How long are you going to be here?" asked Mr. Green, beginning to accept that perhaps there was no way out of this predicament. "Not six months, I hope."

"*Non, non, non,*" said François (which is French for "no, no, no"). "I will be here for twelve months. I am on the advanced program."

"Twelve months!" exclaimed Mr. Green, truly aghast. "But what am I supposed to do with you?"

"Just treat me as you would your own children," said François.

"He's going to wish he stayed in Belgium," predicted Michael under his breath.

Mr. Green would have dearly loved to send François packing, but after fetching the contract and reading the fine print three times, he realized he could not. If he wanted his children to go to Nicaragua, he had to host the Belgian boy. But Mr. Green reasoned that one foreign child had to be better than three of his own (it was just a case of simple mathematics to his mind), so he decided to stick to his decision. Once Derrick, Samantha, and Michael were safely in Nicaragua, perhaps there would be some way he could lend François out to a sweatshop or a chimney-sweeping service or some such.